A Match Made for Thanksgiving

Holidays with the Wongs, Book 1

Jackie Lau

First edition: October 2019

Print ISBN: 978-1-989610-39-8

Editor: Latoya C. Smith, LCS Literary Services

Cover Design: Flirtation Designs

Chapter 1

"When will you be home for Thanksgiving?" Nick's mother asked. "We're doing dinner on Saturday this year, remember?"

As he held the phone to his ear, Nick Wong looked out at the spectacular view of Toronto from his penthouse. This was his home now. He did not want to go to Mosquito Bay. He'd left the small town on Lake Huron as soon as he'd finished high school and hadn't looked back.

Seriously, it was called *Mosquito Bay*. Why would anyone want to go there?

"Nick?" his mother prompted.

He sighed. "I'll be there by four on Saturday."

"Don't be late. Not like last time."

"I'll do my best."

To be honest, he was sort of looking forward to seeing his family, but he was dreading it at the same time. His family was a bit...much, that was all.

Nick liked to do his own thing. Be his own man. Be in charge.

But in Mosquito Bay, his control seemed to slip away. There were his parents, his white mother and Asian father, who had been high school sweethearts and were confused as to why, at the age of thirty-two, Nick had yet to settle down and have four kids, like they had. Then his father's parents, Ah Ma and Ah Yeh, who were pushing ninety but still surprisingly good at interfering in his life. Well, that was mostly Ah Ma. Ah Yeh, Nick's grandfather, was more interested in ordering things on Amazon—he thought online shopping was the pinnacle of human achievement. He would also make his famous noodles for Thanksgiving.

Nick was already salivating at the thought of those noodles.

"Do you want me to bring the usual char siu?" he asked.

"Yes, please," Mom said.

"Will do. See you next weekend."

"Nick, are you getting off the phone already? I haven't had a chance to ask you any questions."

"You asked when I'd be coming back for Thanksgiving."

"You know what I mean! How's life in Toronto? How's your job?"

They talked for fifteen minutes, and then Nick said, "Sorry, I have to go."

"Hmph. Sure, get drunk and pick up women, then nurse your hangover with dumplings and bubble tea."

"Thanks for your insightful description of my life."

"See you next weekend, Nicky. Love you."

"Love you, too," he said before ending the call.

Alright, time to get his Friday night started. It was six thirty—still very early, but he needed to get out. He'd have a drink or two at Lychee before he met up with Trystan.

Work hard, party hard. Enjoy all the delicious food and women the city had to offer.

Why would he live in Mosquito Bay when he could live in Toronto?

Lily Tseng was boring. It was just a fact.

She'd always known it. It shouldn't have been a shock when her ex broke up with her because she was dull and bland.

Yet when he'd said those words, it *was* a shock.

They'd been together for a year. Surely he hadn't been bored the whole time?

Anyway, she'd turned thirty last month, and it was time to make a change. Next weekend, she'd attempt skydiving and bungee jumping.

Ha! No. She never even dreamed of doing such things.

But tonight, maybe she'd have her first one-night stand.

In the past few weeks, she'd spent a lot of time scoping out possible venues to meet men. She had no interest in going to a club. Not her scene, and she wouldn't venture *that* far out of her comfort zone. Instead, she'd focused on stylish downtown bars and had settled on Lychee. It was a restaurant owned by some up-and-coming Chinese-Canadian chef who'd won a cooking show last year, and it was located on Elizabeth Street, near the former location of Lichee Garden, a well-known Chinese restaurant in decades past—hence the name.

In addition to the main dining area, Lychee had a bar and lounge with eight-dollar cocktails before eight. Lily had peeked in a couple times, and it looked like it had a decent crowd of young, attractive men in suits.

She really did like men in suits.

But maybe all this preparing for her one-night stand defeated the purpose. She was planning it the way she planned everything else in her life. Wasn't part of her goal to be more spontaneous?

Lily sighed and stirred her drink with the straw. She wasn't very good at this.

She was sitting at the bar in Lychee now, waiting for her friends Tara Kim and Sam Rubenstein to show up, but she didn't expect them for another half hour.

That was Lily. Always early.

It was a lovely space, she had to admit. Wood, chrome, and exposed brick that somehow went together just right. High ceilings.

And her drink was delicious. It had black tea-infused vodka, mango juice, lime, and...some other things. She'd forgotten what, but she didn't care. She was just trying her best not to drink it too quickly.

She crossed her legs and smoothed out her red dress. A special dress that she'd bought for this occasion, with Tara's help. It showed more cleavage than she'd normally be comfortable with, but Tara had convinced her it looked smashing, and Lily had to agree.

Now she needed a guy.

What if she didn't find anyone suitable tonight?

Oh, come on, Lily, it's not even seven o'clock. You have lots of time.

She was eager to cross "one-night stand" off her list, though. She loved crossing things off lists. Though perhaps she shouldn't have a list for learning how to be more fun and less boring.

But even if she found a suitable guy—attractive, no creepy vibes, those were the main criteria—how would she approach him? What would she say?

I, Lily Tseng, sensible accountant, am trying to have my first one-night stand. Will you sleep with me, please and thank you?

Dear God. She was hopeless.

She had a sip of her cocktail and looked around. At the other end of the bar, there was a group of men who were a few decades older than her. Next to them were a couple of men closer to her age, but they gave off douchebag vibes.

Nobody made her want to take a second look.

And she was just looking for a potential guy! She hadn't even tried to talk to anyone yet.

"Why is it so difficult to have a one-night stand?" she muttered.

Maybe she should cancel Operation Get Laid Tonight.

"What did you say?"

She startled at the unfamiliar male voice, and a little orange liquid sloshed over the edge of her glass.

"Sorry. Let me get that."

A large hand wiped the spill away with a paper napkin. She looked from the hand to a wrist with an expensive watch, up an arm sheathed in a gray suit jacket and...

Oh.

Her mouth fell open, but she promptly snapped it shut so she didn't look stupid.

Although it was hard not to stare.

The man had nearly black hair with a hint of a wave that made him look roguish, if that was a word anyone used anymore. He had dark brown eyes, a teasing smile, and he caused a pleasant hum in her body, even more so than the delicious cocktail. He looked ever so slightly like Henry Golding.

And he was standing right next to her and—

"Did you ask why it was so difficult to have a one-night stand?" he inquired politely.

—and he'd heard her say that.

Right.

Normally, she was a fairly put-together person who always thought before she spoke, and yet she'd muttered that under her breath when *he* was right next to her.

Though she was trying to act less like herself tonight.

But she wished he hadn't heard. Her cheeks heated in embarrassment, and they heated even more as his gaze slid from her face down to her chest, down to her silver stilettos, the ones she hardly ever wore because they were so high and not at all sensible.

And then, she did something even more shocking.

"Are you offering?" she asked.

She didn't say it with a sassy flick of her hair, nor did she reach out and trail her finger down his arm, but she said those words all the same.

Oh, God. She covered her mouth.

He chuckled and it reverberated in her chest.

"One-night stands are my specialty," he said, "but let's get to know each other first. Can I buy you another drink?"

Was this happening?

This was really happening.

It was probably best that she stop after one drink.

"Um, I'll just have some juice," she said. "Mango, if that's possible." The mango juice in her cocktail had been excellent.

"Maybe some food? The char siu sliders are quite good."

"Sure."

The stranger got the attention of a bartender and placed their order, and a few minutes later, Lily had a glass of mango juice, garnished with a cherry. It probably cost six dollars, and there wasn't even any alcohol.

She pushed aside that annoying voice in her head and sipped her juice.

"What's your name?" she asked.

A one-night stand with a man whose name she didn't know sounded extra naughty, but she couldn't do it. She needed to call him *something*.

"Nick."

"I'm Lily."

He sat down on the barstool next to her, then shrugged out of his suit jacket. He rolled up his sleeves, and the sprinkling of dark hair on his forearms was so damn erotic, for some reason.

Lily squeezed her legs together. She wasn't used to being this physically affected by a man.

Yes, he was perfect for Operation Get Laid Tonight.

She couldn't help feeling a little surprised that he seemed interested in her. Not that she was unattractive—she thought she looked quite good in this outfit, in fact—but he really was *that* sexy. Surely he could have almost any woman he wanted. Why, there was a group of three women on the other side of the bar who were looking in his direction.

"I've never done this before!" she blurted out.

"Done what?"

"Tried to pick someone up at a bar. Had a one-night stand."

He chuckled again, all cool, not flustered like she was.

"You're doing fine," he said, then had a sip of his Old Fashioned.

His drink had a single large ice cube, and she was stupidly amused by it. The ice cube was just so...big. They must have used a special mold to make it.

"What do you do for work, Lily?"

Ooh, she quite liked the way he said her name.

"I'm an accountant at a large engineering firm. And you?"

"Oh, I work in advertising," he said vaguely.

She suspected he had an important position. Management or something.

She didn't ask for details, though. It was only one night; she didn't need to know much about him.

A server set a plate with three char siu sliders in front of them, and Lily suddenly realized she was quite hungry. She picked up the first one. Egg bun, from the looks of it, with barbecued pork, cilantro, pineapple, and some kind of sauce. She attempted to take a dainty bite. It wasn't the sort of food that lent itself to dainty bites, but she tried her best.

"Good?" Nick asked.

She held up a finger. She wasn't quite finished chewing.

"Yes," she said at last. "Very good. You were right."

He picked one up, and she watched his Adam's apple as he swallowed, wondering why she'd never been so captivated by a man's throat before.

Maybe it was just Nick's throat. Hmm. She wanted to kiss it right...there.

"You want the last one?" He motioned to the plate.

"Mm. Yes, please."

"Will you be this polite later?" he asked, leaning closer.

A sizzle of energy traveled down to her toes.

Oh, she liked this. She couldn't remember the last time a man had talked to her this way.

She grinned. "May I touch your thigh, please?"

His eyes seemed to darken, and he held her gaze as he laced his fingers in hers and brought their hands to his muscular thigh.

She ate the last slider with her other hand, then chased it down with some mango juice.

"You can touch me wherever you want," he said. "I promise I'll like it all." He paused. "You said you'd never had a one-night stand. Why do you want to have one now?"

"I'm trying new things. Stepping out of my comfort zone. I have a list."

Nick tried not to laugh.

"Of course you have a list," he murmured.

"Why do you say that?" Lily asked. "You only just met me."

True, but he felt like he'd known her for more than twenty minutes, even though that was all it had been. When he'd seen her sitting alone in that incredible red dress, he'd been struck by the way she carried herself with such poise. Everything about her appearance was perfect, not a hair out of place.

He desperately wanted to mess it up.

Then she'd made that comment about a one-night stand, and he'd instantly gotten hard.

When she spoke, she was honest, straightforward, not quite as poised as her appearance would suggest—he wondered if she was like this with everyone. And she got an adorable flush when she was embarrassed.

"You just seem like a list person," he said. "I can't explain it."

"Well, lists are amazing. There's nothing like the satisfaction of crossing something off your to-do list."

"Nothing? Nothing at all?" He stroked the back of her hand with his thumb.

Her pretty red lips parted.

"Why did you pick tonight for your one-night stand? Has it been a while for you?"

"Six months, which actually isn't that long to me, but I was..."

"Horny?" he supplied.

"Yeah. That."

"Say the word."

"No! Not here. Plus I've always hated that word. It makes me think of monsters."

"Monsters?"

"Yeah. Monsters with lots of horns."

He bit back a laugh.

Lily squirmed in her seat, and he hoped that was because she was *horny*, but more likely, she was embarrassed again.

"Okay," he said. "I won't repeat it. You felt...like fucking." He danced his fingertips over her thigh, and she shifted closer to him, her hip pressing against his. "Will you say that word?"

"I only swear around certain people."

"Certain people?"

"My friends. I don't swear with strangers. Or colleagues. Or family."

"You said you want to try new things."

"I do."

"So swear in front of someone you just met. Me."

"That was a fucking good char siu slider."

He laughed. "Now say it in another way. You haven't had sex in a while, and you feel like fucking tonight."

"Alright." She cleared her throat. "Nick, I would like you to fuck me. Please."

Oh, she was killing him.

He wouldn't meet Trystan tonight. When he and Lily left Lychee, he'd take her straight home, and he couldn't help but anticipate her look of delight when she saw his place. The view, the bed. He looked forward to introducing her to *fucking* someone she hardly knew, and tomorrow he could...

He pushed that thought aside. It was a one-night stand, and he was glad that had been clear at the outset. Sometimes he saw a woman more than once—it wasn't *always* a one-night stand with him—but nothing that could be described as more than a fling. Much to the frustration of his parents, he liked his bachelor lifestyle here in the city.

So, no, he wouldn't be introducing Lily to a whole bunch of new experiences.

He shrugged off his curious twinge of disappointment and rested his hand on her thigh, pushing up her knee-length skirt just a little so he could touch her skin.

"Thank you for propositioning me," he said. "I accept. But you are free to change your mind at any time, okay?"

She nodded and had a sip of her mango juice.

He was getting jealous of that red straw.

He leaned forward and pressed a kiss to the top of her neck. She was as sensitive as he'd imagined. Then he worked his way along her jaw, planting a kiss to her chin before claiming her mouth.

She tasted sweet, of mango and pineapple, and he pulled her closer so he could taste her more fully.

"Nick," she said. Quietly, but he still heard it above the background noise in the bar.

"Lily?" another female voice said.

She jumped away from him and looked at the two women behind them, one East Asian and the other white.

"Please continue," the Asian woman said, smirking. "Don't mind us."

"It's not what it looks like!" Lily said.

He put his hand on her shoulder. "Lily, I think it's exactly what it looks like."

"Right. Well." She gestured to the two women. "These are my friends, Tara and Sam, and this is Nick. We, um, just met."

Sam—the white woman—held up her hand for a high five, but Lily didn't slap it.

"I didn't think you were serious about meeting a guy at a bar," Tara said. "I should have known you always do whatever you set your mind to, but I thought you'd need some encouragement."

Lily stood up. "You two will be okay without me, won't you?"

"We can hang out with your friends for a while," Nick said. "I don't mind."

He'd prefer to bring her home right now, but it was only seven thirty. The night was still young. He almost never took a woman home before midnight, but it would be nice to have extra time with Lily.

"No, no," she said. "We'll go."

"As you wish." He paid their bill, then stood up and tucked her hand in the crook of his elbow.

Sam was staring at them, her mouth hanging open.

"Don't worry, we'll find someone else for you." Tara tugged her along. "Lily, remember to text me, okay?" she said over her shoulder.

Lily nodded.

And then Nick was alone with Lily, and they had a whole night ahead of them.

Chapter 2

"WHAT THE FUCK," LILY said under her breath as she took in the view from Nick's living room. "What the fuck."

He definitely had an important job if he could afford a place like this. It was a penthouse on the fifty-third floor of a new building downtown, only a short walk from Lychee, thank God, and everything was sleek black and metal. And the view!

When she'd imagined having a one-night stand, she hadn't imagined being with a guy who looked as hot as Nick and who seemed to be a hotshot CEO or something like that. She couldn't help feeling a little inadequate, like she didn't belong in his world, but she'd try to ignore those thoughts and enjoy the night.

This would be quite the memory.

"There you go," Nick said, coming up behind her. "Swearing again."

"It's a view that encourages obscenities," she said.

"Mm. You want anything? Water?"

"No, I'm good."

He was standing behind her, infuriatingly close. Infuriating because she could feel the heat radiating off him, but he wasn't actually touching her, and he hadn't kissed her since they'd been interrupted at the bar.

But tonight, she was a sexy, confident woman, and she could make the first move.

She leaned back against him, and he folded his arms around her. He'd only turned on a light near the door; it was still mostly dark here, aside from the lights of the city. Just the two of them, and this night that felt like a dream.

He'd probably done this with lots of women. *One-night stands are my specialty.* She tried to push that out of her mind. She didn't care what he did on any night but tonight, and tonight, he was with her. They would use protection. It would all be fine. She'd texted Tara his address and phone number, just in case.

He kissed the crook of her neck.

"You're beautiful," he breathed, leaning down to rest his chin on her shoulder.

"I'm nervous," she said, which wasn't the way she usually responded to a compliment.

"We don't have to do it."

It. *Sex.* Something she'd only ever done within a relationship, but she wanted this night with him.

He really was a very nice man. In her mind, she gave herself a high five for making such a good choice. She felt safe, safer than she'd thought she would feel with someone she hardly knew.

"I want to," she said. "I very much want to."

"Say it again. Like you did at the bar."

"Nick, I would like you to fuck me."

"You forgot the 'please'."

"Please."

"It would be my pleasure." He pulled her closer and rubbed himself against her.

She gasped. He was—

"Feel how hard it makes me when you talk like that."

Stupidly, it made her think of the ice cube in his Old Fashioned, the ice cube that was a bit bigger than any ice cube she'd ever seen before.

"Don't worry," he murmured. "I'll take good care of you."

She continued to stare out the window as he pressed himself against her and ran his hand under the hem of her dress and up her thigh.

"Okay?" he asked, the tips of his fingers inside the waistband of her panties, the lacy black ones she'd bought for tonight.

"Yes." She pressed herself back against his cock.

His fingers dipped inside her underwear, running over her slit and casually stroking her.

"It's a very nice view, isn't it?" he said. "That's part of the reason I got this place. Good location. Lovely view."

"Gunh." She was unable to form proper words.

With his other hand, he undid the zipper at the side of her dress and slid one thin strap down her shoulder. He slipped his hand inside her strapless bra and gently kneaded her breast as he planted kisses up and down her neck.

She was drowning in sensations.

He pushed a finger inside her. An intimacy she'd never allowed a man she'd only met an hour before, but the fact that she hardly knew him made her blood pump quicker.

Lily needed to kiss him. Properly this time, now that it was just the two of them.

She turned in his arms, and he kept his hand inside her panties as she set her lips to his. His mouth was soft and warm and overwhelming, especially with everything else he was doing to her.

She could lose herself in this kiss.

When he deepened the kiss, his tongue touching hers, she unbuttoned his shirt in a hurry and moved her fingers over his chest. Exploring. Making a memory she'd never forget.

He hissed out a breath.

When she undid his belt and pants and slid her hand inside his underwear, he did it again.

She wasn't nervous anymore. No, just eager.

Lily wrapped her hand around his cock. Ooh, yes, that was nice. She slid her hand up and down, ran her thumb over the bead of precum at the tip.

"Nick, I—"

She squeaked in surprise as he lifted her onto the couch. He pulled off her panties and raised her skirt, baring her to him, and then he set his mouth on her.

His very talented mouth.

She'd always loved oral sex, and it was the one way she could reliably orgasm, but he put all of her previous boyfriends to shame. And the curtains were wide open in front of them! The whole city could watch her being pleasured!

Except it was dark in here, and they were on the fifty-third floor.

But it gave her a thrill to be able to see the city before her as a man had his head between her legs.

He slipped one finger inside as he licked her, and she bucked against him.

"More," she panted.

He gave her more, adding a second finger and sucking on her clit.

And then she was coming for him, this man she hardly knew, and it felt like she was letting go of all the times she'd played it safe, all the times she'd been the good daughter rather than having fun.

She was free.

She said his name quietly, but she shook and soared like never before.

He lifted his head and smiled lazily at her, then picked her up and carried her to another room. He set her down on a bed and flicked on the lights, giving her a better look at him.

When he slid off his shirt, exposing all of his chest and arms, it was a magnificent sight. Once again, she congratulated herself on making such a good choice for a one-night stand, though it was still hard to believe this was actually happening.

Next, he pushed down his pants and boxer briefs. His cock jutted out, and he pumped it a few times.

Dear God. She breathed rapidly as she stared at him.

Nick climbed onto the bed and crawled toward her. Predatory, but like a very friendly predator, and she chuckled at that thought.

"What?" he asked.

"Nothing," she said.

He pulled her dress over her head. "You are stunning, Lily." He said it solemnly, but she caught a hint of a smile before he leaned down and kissed her as he pressed his hand between her legs once more.

He kissed her leisurely for a while, the expanse of his skin against hers, and then his kisses became sloppier, more desperate. She squirmed beneath him.

"God, I want you," he murmured. "You ready?"

"Yes. Do you have a condom, or should I get my purse?"

He picked up a condom from the night table and quickly rolled it on. "I think I'd like you in this position."

The next thing she knew, she was on all fours, her ass in the air.

"Is that okay?" he whispered.

She nodded.

She'd take him any way he wanted, if only he'd ease the ache inside her.

He knelt behind her and pressed the tip of his cock to her entrance. Slowly, he eased himself inside, and she gasped. Soon, he was all the way in, and he was big, yes, but she could take him, no problem.

"Okay?" he asked.

"You feel amazing," she said.

He started to move, in and out, and nothing mattered but her pleasure.

He leaned down and kissed the side of her neck, fondled her breasts with one hand, and it was all she could do just to keep breathing. She couldn't even hold herself up on her hands and knees anymore; she slid down so she was lying on her stomach.

And still he fucked her and kissed her neck.

"You're incredible," he whispered. His breath tickled her, made her break out in goose bumps. She pushed back against him, wriggled her ass. "Yes, that's good. Take it, Lily."

He pulled out of her, much to her dismay, but only so he could roll her onto her back, and then he was inside her again. He held her gaze as he licked his finger, then brought his hand down and touched her clit.

The pleasure was so sharp that she nearly flung herself off the bed. Pressure built up inside her, and everything in her contracted then expanded for a long, glorious moment.

Nick growled and picked up his pace, finishing inside her as she came down from her high.

One-night stands were *awesome*.

Nick pulled on his boxer briefs and climbed back into bed with Lily.

"Hey, you." She giggled and pulled him against her, and he was happy to oblige.

"Hey," he said. There was an unfamiliar sensation in his chest as he wrapped his arms around her.

They lay in silence for a minute, and he idly stroked her hair. It was silky and long, well below her shoulders, and smelled faintly of something floral. He wasn't sure what, but he liked it.

"So what happens now?" she asked.

"What do you mean?"

"In a one-night stand. I thought you were the expert."

"Well, we might do it again or go to sleep." He glanced at his alarm clock. "It's only nine o'clock, so we're about four hours ahead of schedule. If you want, I can get a taxi, and you can go home or join your friends."

She jerked up to a sitting position. "You want me to leave?"

Her disappointed expression was so guileless.

He bit back a smile. "No, I just thought you might prefer to, so you didn't have to spend the night, but I'd be more than happy to have you stay."

Yes, he very much wanted to do that again. Once hadn't been enough.

"Could we get some food first?" she asked. "Maybe bubble tea, too. I'm craving it."

He laughed. "I know just the place."

They got dressed and headed outside. It was early October, cool enough for a light jacket but still pleasant.

He led her to a nearby bubble tea shop on Dundas, where she got an oolong milk tea with tapioca pearls, and he got a taro milk tea.

This was what he loved about Toronto. He could walk outside his condo and have so many different kinds of food and drink within ten minutes. There were endless choices. Whereas in Mosquito Bay, there were only a handful of restaurants and one bar.

No, this was the life.

He and Lily moseyed onward. She looked so radiant right now, and *he* was the reason for that. He had a strange impulse to hold her hand, but he quashed it.

It was unusual for him to be out with a woman like this, wandering about with a drink in hand. They'd already had sex, and they would do it again, but there was no rush. He'd simply enjoy being with her.

"Here." He led her down a side street, to a cramped dumpling shop called XLB. "Don't worry, they're fast. Six soup dumplings for three bucks. What do you think?"

Her eyes widened. "Six for *three* bucks? In that case, I'll have twelve."

Fifteen minutes later, they were sitting on a bench in the park behind the art gallery, eating their juicy soup dumplings from take-out containers, their bubble tea nearly finished.

"These are delicious," Lily said before putting another one in her mouth. "I've never heard of this place before. I'll have to go back."

"The best cheap xiaolongbao you can get," he said. "Not the very best I've had, but very good for the price."

She smiled at him, her face lit by the nearby streetlight.

"So," she said, "any plans for Thanksgiving next weekend?"

He felt momentarily disoriented, but she was just making pleasant conversation.

"I'm going to my hometown to see my family," he said. "Where there are no dumplings or bubble tea, and I'll be itching to escape as fast as possible."

"Same here." She chuckled. "Where is your...never mind."

Yes, there was no sense in talking details, not when they were just together for a night.

This was different from a regular one-night stand, though. It felt almost like a dream.

God, he was losing it.

His phone chirped. "Sorry, I should get that. Could be work."

"No worries. Go ahead."

It wasn't work. No, it was a message from Greg, asking who was bringing the char siu home for Thanksgiving.

"Anything important?" she asked.

"Nah, just my older brother." Whom he wouldn't give another thought to tonight.

After she disposed of the containers, he pulled her onto his lap. He wound her hair around his hands and kissed her until she was breathing quickly and her face was flushed.

He loved how she responded to him.

She rubbed herself against his erection, only the thin fabric of her panties covering her.

He groaned and stood up. "That's it. Time to take you back to bed."

And that was exactly what he did.

When he was lying in bed afterward, listening to Lily's rhythmic breathing as she slept, he realized he'd almost perfectly followed his mother's description of his life: he'd picked up a woman and had dumplings and bubble tea. Not to nurse his hangover—he hadn't drunk much today—but it was a horrifying realization nonetheless.

Still, he couldn't regret tonight. It was the best night he'd had in a long, long time.

Lily walked out into the sunshine with a big smile on her face.

It was ten o'clock in the morning, and she was wearing the same dress as the night before. Although she'd cleaned up her make-up and run a brush through her hair, she looked a touch bedraggled.

Walk of shame?

Ha!

She was on cloud nine.

After dumplings and bubble tea, they'd had sex twice more at Nick's place before going to sleep. He'd suggested she sleep naked, but she'd insisted on borrowing a shirt. A plain white T-shirt that smelled deliciously like him.

This morning, she'd woken up to find him lounging in bed next to her, working on his laptop, but he'd set it aside the instant she sat up, then made love to her again.

Made love?

What was she talking about? It had been sex, plain and simple. Damn good sex.

Really, she needed to have one-night stands more often. She suspected they wouldn't all be this amazing—she'd just gotten lucky her first time—but still.

She pictured going to another bar and meeting a man who looked suspiciously like Nick. It was hard to think of anyone else right now. When she'd stepped out the door, she'd nearly asked if she could see him again, but then she'd snapped her mouth shut.

That was part of the magic: it was only one night. One perfect night.

There was a hollow feeling in her heart, but she pushed it aside and held her head high. She'd had sex four—four!—times in twelve hours. Nick was gorgeous and talented, but also kind and attentive, and he'd made her eggs and toast and coffee for breakfast *while wearing only his underwear*. Like some kind of fantasy man, except he was utterly real, and he'd wanted her.

A great night, sure, but this was for the best. She couldn't imagine he'd want anything long-term with her anyway. If one-night stands were his thing, he probably got bored easily.

Her phone rang, interrupting her thoughts. There was only one person who would call—not text—at ten in the morning on the weekend.

"Lily!" her mother shouted. "I have a surprise for you!"

Dear God. A surprise from her mother. This could be anything. Hopefully just some kind of face cream. "What is it?"

"Next weekend, don't come here for Saturday dinner, okay?"

"Why not?"

Ma was giggling. Actually giggling. "You have a date!"

Oh, no.

No, no, no, no.

It must be because Lily had recently turned thirty.

She hadn't been allowed to date in high school. When she'd started university at Western, that had changed to, "As long as it doesn't affect your grades, even a little." When she'd gotten her job in Toronto, her mother had said that she should focus on her career for a few years and there would be time for men later, but as long as it didn't affect her work, it was fine.

And then when she'd turned twenty-eight, her mom had demanded to know why she hadn't gotten married yet.

Since then, her mother would occasionally bring up a man and suggest Lily give him a call or look him up on "that book of faces thing."

Ma knew it was actually called "Facebook" but seemed to enjoy when Lily and her younger sister rolled their eyes.

But now, Ma was getting more involved than casual suggestions here and there. Now she was *setting up dates* for her daughter.

Lily, however, was happily single for the time being. Not like she'd sworn off relationships, but she enjoyed the chance to do things like have a hot one-night stand.

Her mother would be scandalized if she could see Lily now, walking to the subway in a slightly wrinkled dress and silver stilettos.

Lily was, after all, the good daughter.

"No, that's quite alright," she said. "I can take care of my own dating life, thank you."

"That is what I thought for many years, but now you are thirty and no man! It is time to take things into my own hands."

"No, Ma, I—"

"His name is Greg," Ma said. "He is an engineer, and he lives in Toronto, like you! I know his parents. I told them you will come to their Thanksgiving dinner next Saturday."

This wasn't just a date. It was some kind of meet-the-family nonsense that involved Thanksgiving dinner. No, she didn't need this.

In fact, she was speechless with the horror of it.

"His father is Chinese," Ma continued. "Cantonese, but—"

"Ma! No."

"Yahui..."

Oh, no. This was bad. Ma had brought out Lily's Chinese name, something she wielded with great care. She only did this when she *really* wanted Lily to do something. It was a sign that she would not back down.

Lily could argue, but the amount of time and energy she put into protesting would be more than she'd need to attend this so-called date. If her dad were still here, she might have appealed to him for help, but...

Her heart clenched at the memory of her father, and then she felt guilty about not wanting to do what her mother asked.

"They have four children," Ma said. "Three sons, one daughter, and they are setting them all up for Thanksgiving as a surprise."

Lily couldn't help laughing. Poor Greg and his siblings.

It was a relief to know there would be other dates present, though. Less pressure on her. Hopefully it would be entertaining, but it would probably veer into downright painful pretty quickly.

"Alright," she said with a sigh. "I'll do it."

But that didn't mean she had to look forward to it.

No, instead she was looking forward to the next time she got to have a one-night stand, preferably with someone just like Nick.

She doubted this Greg person would be anywhere near as attractive as Nick.

It was pretty unlikely, wasn't it?

Chapter 3

Nick pulled up to the old brick house where he'd spent his childhood and released a breath as he put the car in park.

Suitcase in hand—his mother always insisted he stay overnight—he walked up the driveway and opened the front door, which was never locked. As he took off his shoes, his brother ambled over.

"Hey, man," Zach said, slapping him on the back. "Good to see you."

Zach was the third sibling, the only one who'd stayed in Mosquito Bay. He worked as a science teacher at the local high school they'd all attended back in the day.

"How was the drive?" Zach asked.

"Oh, not bad. Bit slow coming out of Toronto, but I can't complain."

"Who's that?" yelled their mother from the kitchen.

"Nick's here!" Zach shouted back.

The next thing he knew, there was a stampede to the front hall, Mom and Dad in the front, and Ah Ma and Ah Yeh hobbling behind them.

"Nicky!" His mother threw her arms around him. His father was next and gave him a more restrained hug.

"Ah, Nicky!" Ah Ma said. "You stop bossing people around in the city long enough to visit us. How nice of you. We have a big surprise."

"A big surprise?" Nick said as she patted his back. She didn't come up to his shoulder. "What is it?"

"It's a *surprise.*" Mom turned to her mother-in-law. "You weren't supposed to say anything."

"Okay," Ah Ma said, "there is *not* a surprise. I have been forbidden from talking about it. Now I will go back to the kitchen."

"No!" everyone shouted.

She laughed. "Don't worry, I'm just teasing!"

In Nick's experience, most people thought their grandmothers were amazing cooks. People assumed he ate delicious Chinese food made by Ah Ma all the time.

No.

Ah Ma was, frankly, a pretty terrible cook. When they'd had a restaurant in town, Ah Yeh had done most of the cooking.

Now that the initial excitement of his arrival had passed, Nick brought the char siu to the kitchen, then followed

Zach, Ah Ma, and Ah Yeh into the living room, where Greg was sitting on the couch. He raised his hand in greeting. "Hey."

That was Greg, a man of few words. Never one to get caught up in the excitement of anything because, well, he didn't find many things exciting. He enjoyed model trains and CBC radio—Greg was an old man in some ways—but even then, his enjoyment was more restrained.

Like Nick, Greg lived in Toronto. Sometimes they drove down together, but Greg had wanted to stay in Mosquito Bay for two nights this Thanksgiving, and there was no way Nick was staying more than one.

"Is Amber here yet?" Nick asked.

"No," Zach said, "but you know Amber."

Yes, their little sister was always late.

It was only four o'clock, though, and they probably wouldn't eat until six. There was still plenty of time. Amber lived about an hour away in Stratford, where she worked in marketing at the theater festival.

Nick made himself comfortable on the couch. He could check if his parents needed any help in the kitchen, but based on past experience, they'd either shoo him out immediately or fail to notice his presence because they were making out. Personally, Nick couldn't imagine being with the same person for so long and still wanting to make out like that.

"What's that?" he asked, nodding at a green furry thing on the coffee table.

Ah Yeh leaned forward and picked it up. He put it on his hand.

It was a green puppet, a velociraptor from the looks of it.

"You got that on Amazon?" Nick asked, though it didn't need to be said. His grandfather *loved* buying things from Amazon.

"Of course. You can find everything on Amazon."

"Yes, but why do you need a green dinosaur puppet?"

"For your children, of course."

Nick coughed. "What?"

"My great-grandchildren. I think I will be getting some soon, if today's surprise—"

"Aiyah!" Ah Ma said. "They forbid us from talking about it, weren't you listening?"

Well, this was truly bizarre.

Nick could also make out a very small sweater sitting on one of the end tables. What the hell? Sure, his parents and grandparents had occasionally talked about him and his siblings getting married and having kids of their own, but actually buying things for these hypothetical children seemed a bit much.

"So, what's new in Mosquito Bay?" he asked.

"The diner changed hands," Zach said, "and Mrs. Meyer—remember her? She finally retired."

Zach caught him up on all the news about town, Ah Ma adding her opinions here and there. Ah Yeh fell asleep in his chair. Greg grunted occasionally.

Nick was about to ask Zach how his job was going when the doorbell rang.

"I'll get it," Greg said.

He got up and went to the door, returning to the living room a few minutes later with a woman who definitely wasn't their sister, but she wasn't a stranger, either.

Diana Lam.

The Lams were family friends of the Wongs. Diana was twenty-seven now, if Nick remembered correctly, a year older than Amber. He hadn't seen her in several years.

Strange. Sure, the Lams were friends, but Thanksgiving was always just family. And if Diana was here, where were her parents? It wasn't surprising that her brother, Sebastian, wasn't present, though. Last Nick heard, Sebastian was doing his residency on the other side of the country.

But the rest of her family?

"Hey, Diana," Zach said. "Wasn't expecting to see you today. What's up?"

"I'm your date!"

"My date?"

"Ah, the first surprise is here," Ah Ma said.

Zach turned to their grandmother. "I don't understand."

Ah Ma was grinning evilly, which always heralded bad things.

"You see," she said, "we have a problem. All four of you are grown-up. Thirty-four, thirty-two, thirty, and twenty-six. Yet no one is married. Not even engaged. When your parents were twenty-six, they were already married and had Greg. Rosemary says maybe romance is not for everyone, but out of the four of you, I would think at least three would be interested, yes?"

Nick scrubbed a hand over his face. "So you set us all up for Thanksgiving? That's the surprise?"

"Yes! The woman we found for you is—"

"Don't ruin it!" Mom came into the living room. "You'll meet her when she arrives."

"I don't want to get married, Mom," Nick said, "but Greg does, and he's the oldest. You could have set him up without involving the rest of us."

"Go big or go home!" Ah Ma said gleefully. "That's the expression, right?"

"Besides," Nick continued, "I'm perfectly capable of meeting my own women."

He recalled the woman he'd had in his bed last weekend. He'd thought of Lily many times in the past week. Once, he'd even spaced out for a whole five minutes at work, remembering how it felt to have her legs wrapped around him.

He pushed that thought out of his mind.

"Then why don't you bring these women home with you?" Mom asked.

"He does bring them home," Zach piped up, "but he doesn't think of this place as home."

Mom looked scandalized.

Ah Ma looked confused.

Ah Yeh was snoring in the corner, the velociraptor puppet on his hand.

"What does he mean, Nicky?" Ah Ma tugged his sleeve. "I don't understand."

"He's not serious about any of the women he meets in Toronto," Greg said. "That's why he's never brought them to Mosquito Bay. He just brings them to his bed."

"And why haven't you brought women here, Greg?" Ah Ma asked.

"Greg isn't very good at meeting women," Nick said. "He's too busy grunting in the corner."

"Am not," Greg said...with a grunt.

His brother did have a sense of humor. Sort of.

"So this matchmaking business is good for him," Nick continued, "but not for the rest of us."

"But my life is in Toronto," Greg said, "not Mosquito Bay. I don't need to meet a woman who lives in Mosquito Bay."

"Ah, but your date lives in Toronto!" Ah Ma said. "Very pretty girl. Daughter of your mother's friend."

"You convinced her to come all the way to Mosquito Bay for dinner?"

"She is visiting her family for the weekend. Not so bad a drive from there."

"Hmm," Greg said uncertainly.

"Why did you set me up with the girl who ran an electric train through my hair when I was a kid?" Zach asked.

"I did not do that," Diana said.

"You did so."

"Ah, you are arguing." Ah Ma nodded sagely. "Good, good. This is always, what do you call it? A *prelude* to kissing."

Just then, Amber stormed into the living room, followed by Darren, her boyfriend.

Well, *ex*-boyfriend.

"Darren claims you invited him as my date!" Amber said to Mom. "He's lying, isn't he?"

"No," Mom said, "he isn't."

"They arranged Thanksgiving dates for all of us," Zach said. "Guess you got stuck with one you've already dated."

Amber crossed her arms over her chest. "There is no way I'm having pumpkin pie with that turd of a human being."

"Excuse me?" Darren said.

"I always liked you together," Ah Ma said. "Why did you break up?"

"I am not having this conversation." Amber turned away.

This was going to be interesting.

Nick wondered who they would set him up with, though he couldn't say he was looking forward to his date's arrival. Amber had gotten her ex and Zach had gotten a family friend, so it seemed likely that Nick would get a woman he already knew, too.

He headed to the kitchen, where his father was working on the potatoes.

"You knew about this whole matchmaking plan?" Nick asked.

"Sure," Dad said. "Not that I expected anything to come of it, but I thought it would be entertaining, at the very least."

"And you wonder why I don't come back here more often!"

"That's not fair." Dad set down his knife. "We've never attempted matchmaking on this scale before."

"You've attempted it on smaller scales?"

"Only with Zach, since he lives here."

This was great. Just great. Nick couldn't wait until he could return to Toronto tomorrow, knock back a couple drinks, maybe pick up a woman at a bar. Eat a few Korean tacos, or some other food that didn't exist in Mosquito Bay.

He couldn't help picturing someone who looked like Lily. Why did he keep thinking of her?

The doorbell rang.

"I'll get it," Nick shouted, heading to the front hall.

He opened the door to reveal a young woman, who was smiling hesitantly and carrying a large Tupperware of what looked like Nanaimo bars.

Nick loved Nanaimo bars, but he didn't care, not now. Because this woman, who was wearing jeans and a light pink sweater, was very familiar.

He blinked, trying to clear his mind. He must be imagining this.

But when he opened his eyes, she was still standing there.

Lily.

Chapter 4

Oh, no.

This couldn't be happening.

How was this happening?

Lily was never supposed to see Nick again. It was supposed to be a one-night stand. He was meant to be a pleasant—*very* pleasant—memory, not someone she would ever encounter in real life.

He was wearing a polo shirt and jeans today. She'd always been partial to men in suits, but he pulled off the casual look well, too. And the naked look.

Get it together, Lily!

She should not be recalling when he lifted her onto the couch, spread her legs, and went down on her, without even closing the curtains, and—

Okay, seriously, Lily. Not important right now.

Her face flamed.

She was supposed to be set up with a man named Greg and meet his family. She'd even made Nanaimo bars for this wholesome occasion. And now she'd discovered that she'd already slept with someone in Greg's family. Likely Nick was his brother.

Her only one-night stand! What were the odds?

She couldn't help wishing she'd been set up with Nick instead, but then she felt stupid and naïve. To him, she was probably just another woman he'd spent an enjoyable night with. Whereas he was the man who'd given her the hottest experience of her life.

There was no way she could actually go out with Greg. Not that she'd had high hopes for this matchmaking event—she'd done it to satisfy her mother—but now it was an impossibility. It would be too weird.

She'd just try to get through dinner and hope Nick wouldn't say anything. She didn't want his family judging her.

Well, she didn't mean she wanted him to say *literally* nothing, like he was doing now. He was simply staring at her. Shocked, like she was.

But she'd prefer if he didn't let on that they knew each other.

"Lily," he whispered, "are you my date?"

She shook her head. "Your brother's, I think. Don't say anything, okay?"

He nodded just as another man walked over to the door. The man looked quite a bit like Nick. Maybe an inch or two taller. Good-looking, nice build.

He didn't affect her nearly as much as Nick did, however.

Plus, he was frowning.

Mind you, Nick was frowning now, too, but during the night they'd spent together, he'd smiled at her a lot, aside from the times when he was looking at her intensely, like he wanted to rip her dress off. And when he *was* ripping her dress off.

Stop it, brain!

"Lily, is that what you said your name was?" Nick said.

"Yes. I'm supposed to be Greg's date."

"Hi," said the other man. "I'm Greg."

"Well, um, nice to meet you!"

She couldn't think of anything else to say, not with Nick standing there. It was hard to think clearly in his presence.

"My mom says you're an engineer?" she managed at last.

"Yes," Greg said.

Hmm. He wasn't the greatest conversationalist. No mention of what kind of engineer he was, or anything else.

"I wonder when your date will get here," Greg said to Nick.

"I'm told your parents invited dates for all of you?" Lily said.

"Yep, all four of us," Nick confirmed. "Though I suspect my sister's date will be heading off any minute."

Just then, there was some yelling from another room.

"I never want to see you again!" shouted a woman.

"How did things get so bad so fast?" Lily asked.

"They already know each other," Nick said. "In fact, they used to date, and apparently it did not end well."

He left and came back with his hand grasped around a smaller man's upper arm.

"I don't care that my parents invited you," Nick said. "My sister never wants to see you again, so you're not staying for dinner."

"But..."

Greg opened the door and Nick shoved the man out. He slapped his hands together afterward.

Lily had to admit, the whole thing turned her on a little.

"Ah, who is here?" said a female voice.

Suddenly, there was a whole crowd of people in the front hall, just as Lily was in the process of taking off her shoes.

"You are Lily!" said the elderly woman, presumably Nick's grandmother. "Yes, your mother is right, you are very pretty."

"Uh, thank you."

"Welcome to our home. I'll take those for you." A middle-aged white woman held out her hands, and Lily passed her the Nanaimo bars. "I'm Rosemary, Greg's mother."

"Uh, hi. Nice to meet you."

"This is my husband, Stuart." She gestured toward an Asian man with long, graying hair. He bore a slight resemblance to Nick.

"You can call me Ah Ma," said the elderly lady. "You will be part of the family soon, so you might as well."

"Let's not get too far ahead of ourselves," Rosemary said. "This is just a setup since Greg here isn't very good at meeting women. Like our other sons."

A moment later, the doorbell rang, and Nick opened the door to reveal a petite white woman with wavy blond hair. She wore jeans and an off-the-shoulder floral top.

"You must be Nick!" She grinned, then gave him a hug. "I'm Janice."

Janice had a rather squeaky voice.

Or maybe she didn't, and Lily was just jealous because Janice was touching Nick and she wasn't.

She tried to push those feelings aside. She had no claim on him, and if Nick was genuinely interested in this woman, what was Lily going to do? He was welcome to be interested in any woman he liked. He'd done nothing wrong.

Then he looked at Lily. Was it her imagination, or was that a lustful look in his eyes?

Nah, must be her imagination.

She took a deep breath. This was going to be a long dinner.

·❤·❤·❤·❤·❤·

Nick surveyed the table. There was turkey and stuffing, as well as roasted potatoes, butternut squash, sautéed snow peas, and a large dish of noodles they simply called "Ah Yeh's noodles." Nick had no idea what was in them, but they'd always been his and Amber's favorite, and one year when he was about eight, he'd begged his grandfather to make them for Thanksgiving, and Ah Yeh had done it every year since. There was also lots of cranberry sauce and gravy and warm rolls, plus the char siu he'd brought from Toronto.

It might not be strictly traditional, but in Nick's family, this was tradition, like Pictionary at Chinese New Year.

And this year, they might actually eat most of the enormous quantity of food, since there were three more people than usual.

Lily was sitting next to Greg. He said something to her quietly, and she laughed.

Nick tightened his hand on his fork. Dammit.

Why did his brother get set up with Lily? Why couldn't Nick have been set up with Lily instead? His brother was all wrong for her, that much was obvious. Lily needed someone to add a little excitement to her day-to-day life.

To introduce her to one-night stands and having soup dumplings as a late-night snack.

She and Greg together? It would be dull.

Not that he thought Lily was dull by herself, oh no, but...

Nick gave his head a shake. He was acting like he knew Lily well after they'd spent a grand total of one night together; in truth, he hardly knew her at all.

Except he felt like he did.

He turned his attention back to the woman sitting beside him. Janice was a pig farmer. He had not expected the pint-sized blonde to be a pig farmer, of all things, but she'd taken over the family farm—about twenty minutes from Mosquito Bay—from her father.

Which meant she was totally wrong for Nick.

Despite having grown up in this small town on the shores of Lake Huron, he was very much a city guy, and Janice was committed to her pig farm. She also grew soybeans and corn and was telling him unnecessary details about the crops. Details he was sure someone else would be delighted to listen to.

But he wasn't that guy.

She also seemed to think his family would be particularly interested in soybeans, perhaps because they were Asian? It was a little weird.

"What's that?" she asked, pointing at the char siu.

"Barbecued pork. I brought it from Toronto. Here." He picked up a piece with his fork and placed it on her plate. "What do you think?"

She put it in her mouth and cocked her head to one side. "Not bad."

Not bad? It was the best char siu in Toronto. He'd tried dozens of places over the years he'd lived in the city. This one was the best.

Though the char siu in the slider at Lychee had been pretty good, too. Or maybe that was just the company.

He shot a look across the table. Lily was already looking at him, and her gaze suffused him with warmth.

Jesus, he was losing it.

He'd already slept with her, for God's sake. He shouldn't be this affected by her.

Nick enjoyed a variety of women, had never felt the need to commit to just one. He was young and rich and good-looking, and he enjoyed flirting with new women in bars, dancing with them in clubs. He was always honest about what he was looking for and never led anyone on.

But now, what he wanted more than anything was to sit next to Lily at Thanksgiving dinner. Then he could put his hand on her leg, like he'd done at Lychee, and admire her from up close. Whisper in her ear and hear her laugh just for him.

His parents had done a piss-poor job of matchmaking. Lily made no sense for Greg, and Janice made no sense for Nick. His parents had also done a bad job with Zach and Diana, who seemed to grate on each other's nerves.

Amber, lucky her, was seated next to an empty chair, where Darren should have been, but Amber had gotten so angry at the sight of him that Nick had thrown the bastard out. Why did Mom and Dad think setting her up with an ex was the way to go?

Yes, once this dinner was over, he would make his feelings clear to his parents.

There would be no more matchmaking. End of story.

"So, Lily," Ah Ma said. "What do you do for Thanksgiving in your family? You have turkey?"

Lily shook her head. "One year when I was in elementary school, I begged my parents to have a normal Thanksgiving dinner, like all the other kids. So they bought a turkey, and I'm not sure what went wrong." She chuckled. "But there was lots of yelling, and by nine o'clock that night, the turkey still wasn't done, so we ordered Kentucky Fried Chicken. And that's what we have for Thanksgiving every year now. KFC and an apple pie my mom buys at the grocery store."

"Where did you grow up?" Nick asked.

"Ingleford."

Ah. It was a small town south of London, Ontario if he remembered correctly; Mosquito Bay was to the northwest.

He wanted to ask her more questions. He wanted to know more about her than what kind of bubble tea she liked and how she ate her soup dumplings.

But she was Greg's date.

God, he could barely stand it.

"What about you?" he asked Janice. "You do the whole turkey thing?"

"Yeah. All my extended family. There's twenty-six of us. Or is it twenty-seven now? I keep forgetting."

Nobody said anything for a few minutes, all busy eating their turkey and stuffing and veggies and noodles. Amber, as usual, had loaded up almost entirely on noodles and stuffing. Zach had mostly meat. Greg's plate was perfectly balanced, as always.

Conversation was not flowing naturally.

This, Nick supposed, was what happened when your parents unexpectedly invited dates for all their children. It probably didn't help that he was thinking about how he wanted to rip off his brother's date's pink sweater and feed her Nanaimo bars.

He hadn't eaten a Nanaimo bar in a long time, and he was craving one now.

Did Greg actually like Lily…like that? Or was he just being nice?

Nick and his older brother had never fought over a woman before, perhaps because Greg only occasionally showed interest in anyone and rarely bothered with anything as pedestrian as socializing.

Though he seemed to be doing a good enough job with Lily now.

"Nick, how are things in Toronto?" Ah Ma asked. "You do good business? You trick lots of people into buying things?"

"Thank you for that wonderful description of my job."

"What do you do?" Janice asked. "My parents didn't tell me, just said you were some fancy Toronto businessman."

"I work in advertising."

"Like *Mad Men*?"

"Sure," he said. "Just like *Mad Men*."

"You like living in the city?" She made a face.

"Yeah, I love it."

"Don't you find it noisy?"

"I live on the fifty-third floor. It's not too noisy up there."

"Fifty-third floor?" Janice sputtered. "I'm afraid of heights. What happens if there's a fire? Or a wind storm? What possible advantage could there be to living in downtown Toronto? There's so much traffic. And crime."

"There really isn't. Though the traffic is bad, I'll give you that."

"Hmph."

Nick couldn't stand it anymore. He finished his noodles in a hurry and didn't help himself to seconds—even though he *always* had seconds of Ah Yeh's noodles—and headed to the kitchen.

He needed a break.

Chapter 5

Lily excused herself to go to the washroom, and on the way back, she went looking for Nick. He wasn't hard to find.

He was in the kitchen, eating her Nanaimo bars.

Nanaimo bars were her favorite dessert to make. The bottom was a mix of graham cracker crumbs, coconut, cocoa powder, nuts, butter, egg, and sugar. Next came the creamy filling: butter, cream, sugar, and custard powder. Lastly, the top layer of chocolate.

They were delicious and extremely unhealthy.

But it was Thanksgiving, and she was being forced to sit through a dinner with a family she didn't know. Perfectly nice people, but she felt like she was intruding.

Worse, she had to sit across the table from Nick and his date.

Not that Nick seemed interested in Janice, and it was clear they had nothing in common, but it was hard to watch all the same.

She just...dammit.

Maybe Lily sucked at one-night stands after all and couldn't help getting attached to a man she'd slept with. She was trying to be less boring, but she couldn't truly change the kind of person she was.

Nick turned as she approached. "Do you like him?"

"What?"

"Greg. Do you like him?"

They were whispering, so nobody could hear from the dining room, but something crackled between them. Like a fire on a cold winter's day. There was an unexpected edge to Nick's words.

"He's nice," Lily said, not giving Nick what he wanted.

"Nice," Nick repeated faintly. "He's a little stern and grumpy. Is that the kind of guy you usually go for?"

She shrugged. Greg was perfectly fine, and maybe if she hadn't met Nick first, she would have been interested enough to see him again.

Or perhaps not.

The thing was, she and Greg had no chemistry. Sometimes that developed with time, but it was impossible not to compare him to Nick.

There had been lots of chemistry from the start.

Now he was looking at her with an expression she couldn't decipher. It wasn't an expression she'd seen on him last weekend, when he'd been charming and kind, and then very *purposeful* when he'd started to touch and undress her.

She couldn't help releasing a little squeak at the memory.

Nick plucked a Nanaimo bar out of the container and lifted it to his mouth. She couldn't help staring as he ate.

"These are amazing," he said. "I have no idea what's in Nanaimo bars, but they've always been my favorite."

"Mine, too."

"Yours are especially good."

"I know."

His lips twitched.

"What if I tried to feed one to you?" He took a tiny step toward her.

She breathed in sharply. "You're jealous."

"Very jealous."

"Are you jealous of every woman your brother shows a slight interest in?"

"It's never happened before. I'm not the jealous type. But I still really want you, Lily."

She hadn't expected this.

"How do you want me?" she asked.

"Preferably over the counter."

They were both quiet for a moment, and she could hear laughter and the clink of cutlery from the dining room. She wished they were completely alone.

She squeezed her thighs together.

"It was only supposed to be one night," she said. "I thought you were great at one-night stands. You told me they were your specialty."

"So I did."

"And?"

"You've thrown me off my game."

"Me?"

"Yeah, you."

He reached out and touched her arm; it felt like he was branding her. Then he pulled back and picked up another Nanaimo bar. She'd cut them into small pieces so they could be eaten in a couple bites. He removed the top layer of chocolate and held it to her lips.

"You're not supposed to eat Nanaimo bars like that," she protested. "You're supposed to eat the layers all together. It's the perfect combination." She gestured to his hand. "This is *wrong*."

"There's still a bit of filling, whatever it is—"

"Butter, cream, tons of powdered sugar, and custard powder."

"Don't ruin the magic for me. I don't need to know what's in it."

"I'm not ruining the magic. I know exactly what's in Nanaimo bars, and I still love them." Though knowing the ingredients and quantities made her very conscious of the fact that they weren't healthy.

He held the square of chocolate, with a little of the creamy filling clinging to it, closer to her lips, and she took a bite and chewed slowly. After she finished the chocolate, he held up the rest of the Nanaimo bar, and she licked the filling off the base. Nice and slow.

This wasn't like her.

This wasn't like her at all.

But when his eyes flared with desire, she couldn't deny that it was fun to tease him.

"Okay," Nick said hoarsely. "You've answered the question of what you'd do if I fed you a Nanaimo bar. Now tell me, what would you do if I kissed you? Do you want me to?"

His family was so close, just in the other room. One of those men was her blind date, but it wasn't like he was her boyfriend.

She felt deliciously naughty. She wasn't used to feeling this way, but with Nick...

"I'd like that very much," she said. "I'd like that very fucking much."

He chuckled. "Just like you enjoyed those 'fucking good' char siu sliders last weekend."

"Oh, much more than that."

He stepped closer and rested his hand on her shoulder, and she was overwhelmed by his nearness. His handsome features were mere inches away.

Why wasn't he kissing her yet? Hadn't she already sexily eaten a Nanaimo bar for him?

She needed his lips on hers.

She wasn't used to needing anything this badly. She usually felt restrained, in control, but with Nick, it was different.

Finally, he kissed her, and it was even better than a Nanaimo bar.

His hands stayed firmly on her shoulders. He didn't explore her body, didn't move anything except his lips against hers, but that was enough. It made her feel like she was all that mattered.

He pulled back. "We should head to the dining room. They might wonder where we are."

By the time she'd found her voice, he'd already left, and she leaned against the counter for a moment in a daze.

There was pumpkin pie, apple pie, cherry cheesecake, and Nanaimo bars on the table, plus vanilla ice cream and whipped cream as accompaniments.

Nick enjoyed dessert, but today, he didn't much care.

Sure, he helped himself to a slice of pumpkin pie with a generous dollop of whipped cream, as well as another Nanaimo bar, but all he really cared about was Lily.

Lily, who certainly wasn't going to think about Greg again after that kiss.

She kept catching Nick's gaze, then quickly looking away, as though embarrassed. But when it was just the two of them, she wasn't shy.

They were good together, dammit.

"So, anyway," Janice was saying, "the manure was…"

This wasn't his preferred topic of conversation, especially while eating, and it drove home the point—once again—that they were all wrong for each other.

He could only think of Lily, who was sitting there sweetly across the table from him, focused on her plate of dessert. He wanted—*needed*—to be alone with her again, to feel her shudder at his touch.

"Alright." Zach put his fork down with a clink. "Mom and Dad, why on earth did you set me up with Diana, and Amber with her ex-boyfriend? Why do you feel the need to interfere in our dating lives?"

"We already told you!" Ah Ma said. "Four grandchildren, all single. Clearly you need help."

"No," Zach said, "we don't."

"And Diana is your best friend's little sister."

"Sebastian isn't my best friend. I rarely see him anymore."

"But he was your best friend when you were children, yes?"

"What does that have to do with anything?"

"We did our research." Ah Ma stuffed a bite of cheesecake in her mouth. "Well, mainly Rosemary, because she is the one who reads all the romance novels, but I read a few, too. And this best friend's little sister? We see it in a few books. It always results in a happy ending. So we think, maybe it will work for you!"

Mom turned to Amber. "Sometimes second chance romances turn out well, too, so we figured we'd invite Darren."

"What about Greg and me?" Nick asked. "How did you pick our dates?"

"You and Janice are opposites," Ah Ma said. "Opposites attract, no? And Lily...well, from all I've heard, she sounds like a wonderful woman"—she looked at Lily, who blushed—"and I thought she'd be best with Greg. Though there was that runaway bride..."

"Runaway bride?"

"A new woman in town," Mom said. "Left a guy at the altar. She was supposed to get married again last week, and I thought for sure she'd leave this guy, too, and then maybe she could fall into the arms of one of my sons. But she went through with the wedding. You know Mrs. Meyer? She lost thirty dollars in a bet!"

"Mom," Zach said, "why would you want to set one of us up with a woman who'd left two men at the altar? Seems like a bad bet."

"Aiyah!" Ah Ma said. "Clearly you don't understand these things."

"Clearly not," Greg muttered.

Nick didn't know why his elders were treating their dating lives like they were in a novel, but he didn't bother voicing any complaints. This ridiculous plan of his family's had brought Lily back into his life, and she didn't want Greg the way she wanted Nick.

And Nick was going to...

Well, he didn't know precisely where to go from here. One-night stands were his area of expertise, as he'd told Lily. He didn't know how to do other things, whatever those entailed.

Her tongue darted out of her mouth to lick some whipped cream off her lip, and he nearly growled in frustration. Frustration that he couldn't touch her right now.

All he knew was that he needed more of her.

·❤·❤·❤·❤·❤·

To no one's surprise, Janice and Diana left soon after dinner was over. Nick attempted to help with dishes, but his parents wouldn't let him. They never let him help when he came back to Mosquito Bay for the holidays.

"I'm going to get some fresh air," he said, hoping Lily would understand what he was after.

Indeed, she came out the front door a couple minutes later, and he led her around the side of the house. She had her arms wrapped around herself—it was cooler than it had been earlier.

"Allow me," he murmured. He hauled her against him and replaced her arms with his, holding her close.

She felt amazing; she felt *right*.

Geez, he was having some weird thoughts tonight.

She slid her arms around his neck, tilted her head up, and pressed her mouth to his, just once. "I feel so naughty."

"Mm." He couldn't speak; he was too busy burying his face in the crook of her neck. There was one particular spot that he'd found last weekend, right—

"Ohh."

Yes, right there.

He hoisted her up, his hands under her denim-clad ass. He'd loved her in the red dress, but he also loved her like this, in jeans and a sweater, her back against the brick wall of his childhood home. He set his lips to hers.

"Nick," she said, "what are we—"

"Nick!" someone else shouted. "What are you doing?"

It was Ah Ma.

Chapter 6

Suddenly unsupported by Nick's hands, Lily fell to the grass, unable to get her legs underneath her in time. He'd dropped her the moment he'd seen his grandmother standing before them.

Dear God, they'd been caught.

When she was younger, Lily's sister, Marla, had been caught sneaking out of the house multiple times, sneaking a boy into her bedroom, smoking pot, and many other things.

Lily, on the other hand, had only been discovered while eating Oreos in the middle of the night at the age of eight. That was all.

Oh, she'd also taken an extra box of Pocky from the pantry.

Once.

She'd certainly never been caught in the middle of a make-out session by the man's grandmother. This was a totally new experience, one she wished she weren't having.

She took Nick's extended hand, and he pulled her up to standing.

"I'm so sorry," he said. "You okay?"

"Aiyah!" Ah Ma said, grasping Nick's wrist. "I hear stories about how you are—what do you call it? Playboy? Manwhore? Am I saying this correctly?"

Nick made a strangled sound in his throat. "I think you—"

"What happened?" Rosemary and Stuart rushed around the side of the house, followed by Zach and Greg.

"It's not what it looks like!" Lily said.

Which was stupid.

But it was the first thing that came to mind, because that's what Marla had always said when she got caught, though the phrase had never helped Marla get out of anything.

It was also exactly what Lily had said when Tara and Sam found her kissing Nick.

This past week had certainly been something.

"No lying! You were making out." Ah Ma pointed at Nick, then Lily. "Against the wall! I saw it!"

"Your vision isn't that great," Stuart said, placing a hand on his mother's shoulder.

"I know what I saw! Kissing! Nick kissed Greg's date! Playboy! Man—"

"Okay, okay," Nick said, lifting his hands. "Ah Ma is correct."

"Stealing your brother's woman? I raised you better than this."

"What are you talking about?" Rosemary interjected. "*I* raised him."

Zach was smirking, and Greg looked...well, Lily couldn't read him at all. He always wore the same expression.

Nick curled his arm around her waist in a protective gesture. "Lily and I met last weekend, actually, in Toronto. We went on a date."

"A date!" Zach laughed. "You don't date."

Nick shot him a glare. "I had no idea she was coming to our family Thanksgiving, because that was sprung on us without warning."

"Why didn't you say anything earlier?" Rosemary asked.

"It seemed awkward."

"And I told him not to," Lily added.

"You like Nick better than Greg?" Rosemary asked.

"I'm sorry," she said to Greg. "I was going to tell you, if we ever got a chance to have a private conversation. I didn't mean for you to find out like this."

Greg nodded. "No worries."

"Are you sure?"

"It's fine."

"Where did you meet Lily last weekend?" Ah Ma asked Nick.

"At a bar," Nick replied.

"Is it only physical? Or love at first sight? Maybe we did good matchmaking after all, we just set Lily up with the wrong man!"

"I'd call that bad matchmaking," Stuart said, and Ah Ma gave him a look.

"What's going on out here?" Ah Yeh stumbled around to the side of the house, and Stuart steadied him.

"You missed all the excitement!" Ah Ma said. "Nick was making out with Lily! Why are you always napping? You miss all the good stuff."

Ah Yeh waved this off. "I know this already. I saw them in the kitchen earlier. Feeding each other Nanaimo bars."

"And you didn't tell me?" Ah Ma screeched. "We have such boring lives, and you keep the exciting things to yourself? Wah, you are a bad husband!"

"That's enough," Nick said. "Lily and I are going for a walk now, okay? The rest of you are going back inside, and don't you dare even think about following us. I can't believe that has to be said, but it does."

Ooh. Lily rather liked this commanding voice of his.

As well as the thought of being alone with him once more.

·♥·♥·♥·♥·♥·

Nick led Lily to a small park overlooking the beach, Lake Huron a dark shape just beyond. It reminded her of last week, when she'd seen Lake Ontario from his penthouse.

One week. It had only been one week since she'd met him.

It felt like so much longer.

They sat on a bench. It was a touch cooler by the lake, but when Nick put his arm around Lily, it felt like there was a fire burning inside her.

"Why is the town called Mosquito Bay?" she asked, not feeling like talking about what had just transpired. They were probably due for an important conversation, and she wanted to delay that a little longer.

"No idea. They've tried to change the town name a few times over the years, but it never happened. Sometimes the mosquitos are pretty bad here, but not much different from any of the towns nearby. It's not a big tourist destination, though, despite being on the lake. I once saw it on a list of 'Best Kept Secrets in Ontario'."

"Did you like growing up here?"

He hesitated. "It was fine, but once I was a teenager, it started to feel too small, plus I always felt...different. The town isn't entirely white, but it's still mostly white."

"The other kids used to make fun of my lunches," Lily said. "I was the only Asian kid in my grade. They called me 'Rice Girl.' I knew my food tasted better, but I wanted to fit in, so I pleaded with my mom to make me bologna sandwiches. She refused. When I went to university at Western, there were more people who looked like me, and then I moved to Toronto."

He nodded. "I reinvented myself when I came to Toronto for university. I was determined to be cool for once."

"You weren't the popular and charming quarterback in high school?"

"Nah. I had some friends, but..." He leaned closer. "Don't tell anyone in Toronto. I don't want to ruin my reputation."

His mouth was almost touching her ear. She couldn't think clearly.

She leaned away from him and changed the topic. "There weren't a lot of books about kids like us, either. A few, but not many. I read a lot of the Baby-Sitters Club books. Claudia Kishi—I thought she was great."

Lily felt a moment of embarrassment for admitting her love of that series, but then decided she didn't care, and Nick didn't make fun of her.

It was nice to talk to someone who'd grown up in a place similar to Ingleford. Tara, on the other hand, had grown up in Toronto, and her experience had been very different.

"When did your family come to Mosquito Bay?" Lily asked.

Nick toyed with a lock of her hair. "My grandparents settled here when they arrived from Hong Kong in the sixties. My dad was seven."

"I like your family," she said, but mortification overtook her as soon as she'd spoken. "Though I didn't like it when your grandmother caught us. What was I thinking, Nick?"

"That I'm completely irresistible?" The corner of his mouth kicked up.

She huffed out a laugh. "No, I wasn't thinking at all. I let you kiss me and feed me a Nanaimo bar when your family was just in the other room! In fact, I let you feed me a Nanaimo bar in a totally blasphemous fashion."

"Blasphemous?"

"Like I said, you're supposed to eat the three layers together. Why else did I spend all that time assembling them? If everyone ate Nanaimo bars the way you do, I could have served a bowl of the crust, a bowl of the filling, and a bowl of chocolate."

"Deconstructed Nanaimo bars. Intriguing."

"Totally improper."

"Go out with me, Lily," he murmured. "Let me take you on a date back in Toronto."

She looked at him for a moment, then decided to be completely honest. "I like you, but we lead very different lives. You enjoy going out and partying until four in the morning—"

"I usually shut it down before four. I'm in my thirties now. Two or three is late enough."

"You know what I mean. You live in another world, with your fancy job and your penthouse and your commitment to one-night stands. Me, I occasionally meet up with my friends, but often I'm curled up alone watching a movie on a Saturday night."

"The night we met, it sounded like you were trying to get out of your comfort zone."

"My ex-boyfriend told me I was boring."

"You're not boring." He placed his hand on her cheek, and she melted a little beneath his touch. "You fascinate me."

"Why?"

"You just do."

"Terrible answer."

"Let me take you on a date."

"But you're all about one-night stands, by your own admission. Your brother said as much, too. Yet it sounds like you want more than that?"

"I do."

It baffled her. If someone was going to make Nick change his ways, surely it wouldn't be her. She was an ordinary woman.

"I don't know exactly what I want," he admitted, "but I do want to see you again and go on a date with you."

He smiled at her. It was dark here, darker than walking on the Toronto streets at night, but she could still make out his smile, and oh, it did things to her. Nick was so freaking attractive. She'd hardly been able to take her eyes off him at dinner.

On one hand, going out with him felt like she was playing it safe, as she always had, venturing back into something that might be a relationship.

On the other hand, it felt dangerous to do that with a man like Nick.

"Alright," she heard herself say. "I'll go out with you next weekend, but first, I want you to prove you're serious about me as more than a one-night stand, because I still find it hard to believe."

"What do I have to do?" He leaned forward.

Ooh, her plan was evil. She nearly cackled.

But why was she doing this? She and Nick could just have a fling. Casual sex with no commitments.

Except she knew her feelings would get involved, and it would crush her when it ended. Plus, he was talking about dates, not just sex, and she couldn't help worrying that she wasn't good enough for him.

So she needed some reassurance.

"If you're that serious about me," she said, "then come to my family's Thanksgiving dinner tomorrow."

"To eat Kentucky Fried Chicken and apple pie?"

"Exactly." She felt a little embarrassed about her family's Thanksgiving plans. His family had put out quite a spread, and hers ordered fast food.

But she liked their traditions, and KFC for Thanksgiving had been her father's favorite.

"No problem," Nick said smoothly. "In fact, I'll bake something for dessert."

Her phone buzzed, but she ignored it. "If you like."

"I insist."

He pulled her onto his lap and wound his arms around her waist. There was no family to interrupt them now, and her heart beat quickly in anticipation.

He was about to set his lips to hers when her phone started ringing.

"Oh my fucking God," she said.

Nick laughed.

"Why won't it stop?" How did she answer a phone call? She was drawing a blank. Her proximity to Nick had totally fried her brain.

Finally, she was able to answer the phone.

"Lily," her mother said, "I thought you would be home by now. Are you driving? You shouldn't answer the phone while you're driving."

"I'm still in Mosquito Bay."

"Ah, it's going well! I knew you and Greg would be perfect together. Not that I've ever met him before, but—"

"Actually..." Oh, how did she put this? She couldn't lie, not if her mother was friends with Nick's family, plus she'd asked him to come over. "Actually, I'm getting along well with Greg's brother, Nick. I've invited him over for Thanksgiving dinner tomorrow."

"Greg's brother? I don't understand."

"We already knew each other in Toronto and—"

"You invited him for Thanksgiving?"

Lily had to move the phone away from her ear because her mother was yelling. "Calm down, Ma. Is it okay that he comes over?"

She wasn't sure if her mother was shocked that Lily had easily switched from one brother to the other, or embarrassed that someone else would join in their KFC traditions.

"Of course, " Ma said at last.

Lily spoke to her mother for a couple more minutes as Nick slipped his hands under her sweater and ran them over her stomach, nearly making her miss what her mom said on multiple occasions.

At last, she ended the call, and as soon as she did, Nick's hands were on her breasts.

"Now where were we before my grandma interrupted?" he murmured.

They weren't leaning against a brick wall this time. They were in a public park, but it didn't feel as illicit as being at the side of a man's family's house when she was supposed to be his brother's date.

Nope, everybody knew the truth now. She didn't know exactly where this was going, but there were no secrets anymore.

Nick circled his thumb over her nipple, and she arched against him and felt his erection between his legs. What would it be like to have sex here, in a park by Lake Huron?

No, that was a little too much even for New Lily, who'd picked up a random guy at a bar, then somehow managed to have Thanksgiving dinner with his family.

They kissed for a while. Long, luxurious strokes. He knew how to make her feel so damn good, and when he kissed the base of her neck just...like...that...she was barely even able to breathe.

"Alright," she said when she could take it no more, "I need to leave if I'm going to get home before midnight. It's an hour drive."

"Mm, just a little longer."

"You're a terrible influence."

"That's my goal."

She laughed and kissed him one last time.

"Until tomorrow," she murmured.

Chapter 7

When Nick came downstairs the following morning, he was greeted to a horrifying sight.

Well, "horrifying" might be a bit strong, but it was a sight he didn't really need to see.

His mother was sitting on the counter, her legs wrapped around his father's waist, and they were kissing. A pot of oatmeal was cooking on the stove.

This happened nearly every time he went back to Mosquito Bay. He and Greg would usually stay over for a night or two, and his parents would forget that they no longer had the house to themselves.

"Oh, Smoochie-boo-kins," his mother murmured.

At least, that's what it sounded like, but Nick could have heard incorrectly.

"Ahem," he said. "You're not alone in the house this morning."

Dad stepped back. "Oh, hi, Nick."

"Don't look so scandalized," Mom said. "Old people kiss, too."

"I'm very much aware of that."

An image of him and Lily in their sixties, kissing in the kitchen, popped into his mind.

Nick shook his head. He was getting way ahead of himself. He'd only just decided he wanted something more than a one-night stand, and for him, that was a pretty big deal.

Besides, he'd always been certain he *didn't* want to be like his parents.

But for a moment there...

"You deserve it," Dad said, grinning, "after your grandmother caught you making out with Lily last night."

"She shrieked as though someone had been stabbed," Mom said. "Not that there's been a stabbing in Mosquito Bay in, oh, forty-two years."

"I thought it was thirty-seven years."

"No, I think—"

"Okay, okay." Nick held up his hands. "Enough!"

"Will you have breakfast with us before you leave?" Mom asked.

"Actually, I'm going to stick around a little longer than usual. I won't leave until this afternoon, and then I'm going to Lily's family's Thanksgiving dinner."

Mom and Dad looked at each other.

"Oooh," they said, speaking in unison, as though they'd been together for over forty years. Which they had.

"You and Lily, eh?" Dad slapped him on the back. "And you're meeting her family? This is going fast."

"She's gone through the hardship of meeting my family. Seems only fair."

"Hardship?" Mom clasped her hands to her chest, as though she'd heard terrible news. "*Hardship*? We're nice people."

"Well, sure," Nick said, "but these situations are always awkward. Especially since she came here as Greg's blind date. Anyway, I'm sticking around until this afternoon, and I said I'd bake something for dessert. Maybe those butter tarts you used to make? Or date squares. Actually, you know what? I have lots of time. I'll make both."

Dad turned to Mom. "He really likes her."

Mom just laughed. "You? Baking? You've never baked before, have you?"

"No," Nick said, "but it can't be too hard, once you have the recipe."

"Can you even cook? Do you use the kitchen in that fancy condo of yours? Or are you storing your suits in the oven?"

"Thanks, Mom. Now, where are those recipes, and when does the grocery store open?"

Nick was starting to get the hang of this baking business. He was on his second batch of butter tarts, having burnt the first batch, but this batch was going to work out perfectly, he knew it.

He should have set the timer on the oven the first time, but he'd figured he would notice when it was ten thirty on the kitchen clock, and he would have, except...

Well, the kitchen was a little full.

"Baking is not a spectator sport," he said to his family for the third time.

"Wah, what are you talking about?" Ah Ma asked. "I watch baking and cooking competitions on the television all the time."

"I did not sign up for a baking competition." Nick gritted his teeth. "I just want to bring something nice to my date's family dinner."

"Ah, you are calling her your date, not your girlfriend?"

"I don't like labels."

"Mm, sure, Mr. Fancypants," Mom said.

"Mr. Fancypants!" Zach said. "That's a good one."

"Don't you guys have anything better to do?" Nick muttered.

"No, we really don't," Zach said cheerfully. "What could be better than watching you bake butter tarts for your true wuv?"

Nick did not dignify that with a response.

Zach made smooching noises in the air.

Nick still didn't say anything.

This was the problem with Mosquito Bay. Everyone was all up in everyone else's business, and his family drove him nuts. As soon as he'd mentioned baking, Mom and Dad had called up Zach, Ah Ma, and Ah Yeh and invited them over to watch, despite his protests. Even Greg was watching him bake, though he wasn't saying anything, only occasionally smirking.

Nick shoved the second batch of butter tarts into the oven.

"Look," he said, wiping his hands on the apron that his mother had insisted he wear, "there's nothing weird about a man baking. Dad bakes occasionally, and he does most of the cooking. Ah Yeh is a better cook than Ah Ma."

"Oh, there's nothing weird about a man baking," Dad said. "It's the fact that it's *you* baking."

Everyone nodded in agreement.

"What if it was Greg?" Nick asked as he reached for the container of dates.

Mom shook her head. "Not nearly as exciting."

"But you," Zach said, "with your fancy suits and fancy penthouse and fancy drinks—"

"Thanks for your great description of my life."

"Though I remember Greg baking for Tasha," Zach continued, "and you and I did watch."

"That's right," Nick said. "We watched him make cookies for Valentine's Day back in high school."

Greg grunted.

"I saw Tasha's parents the other day," Mom said. "They told me she's doing well."

Greg grunted again and crossed his arms over his chest.

Excellent. The attention had shifted to Greg. Nick started on the date squares, mixing flour, oatmeal, sugar, baking soda, and salt together in a bowl.

"Why did you drag me here?" Ah Yeh complained to Ah Ma. "I can watch someone bake on the television, no need to leave the house! Or I could be ordering things on Amazon."

"Silly man! We have everything we need. Why buy all this stuff when we already have one foot in the grave?"

"Don't talk like that," Dad said.

"And watching our grandson bake is more exciting than those TV bakers!"

"It really isn't." Nick was now combining the oatmeal and flour mixture with the butter. He was supposed to do this "until crumbly," according to the recipe. Hmm. "Do you think it's crumbly?" he asked his mother.

Which was a mistake. Four people immediately reached for the bowl, ready to put their fingers in and check the consistency of the dough. Or batter.

What was the difference between dough and batter? Did this qualify as either?

Nick had no idea, and he wasn't about to put the question out to his audience.

Fortunately, he managed to move the bowl before everyone could touch it, just as the buzzer on the oven went off. He pulled the muffin pan out of the oven, happy to see the tarts didn't look burnt this time.

"I will help taste test," Ah Ma said.

"No, I will do the honors," Zach said.

"I'm going to have a nap." Ah Yeh headed toward the living room.

"Nobody is trying any of this batch of butter tarts," Nick said. "If you want a butter tart, you can have one of the burnt ones, which were ruined because you're all distracting me."

"I don't want a burnt one," Ah Ma said. "Only the best for me! I am old. One foot in the grave, remember! I must check that the filling is the perfect consistency. It should be a little runny, you know."

"I don't like it runny," Nick protested.

As he finished making the date squares, his family continued to argue about the consistency of butter tart filling. Finally, the date squares were out and cooling, and his family had gotten tired of talking about butter tarts—and, fortunately, had only consumed two between them.

Nick tried a bite, too, and decided they were quite good, though they weren't the best butter tarts he'd ever tasted. That honor belonged to Happy As Pie, one of the bakeries he'd visited in Toronto. He was a bit annoyed, because he wanted the very best for Lily, but considering this was the first time he'd ever baked—and he'd had to contend with his family's interference—he was pretty proud of himself, prouder than he'd been when he'd closed that last deal at work.

Not as proud as he'd been when he'd given Lily all those orgasms last weekend, but still.

He imagined feeding her a butter tart. Breaking off a piece of the crust and popping it in her mouth, then having her lick the filling from his finger. Perhaps she'd be scandalized by the idea of eating the filling and crust separately. Perhaps she'd kiss him afterward and slip her tongue between his lips.

Nick shoved those thoughts aside. He wasn't leaving for Ingleford until four o'clock, and for the next few hours, his main goal was not to let his family drive him crazy, and not to get himself too worked up by the thought of Lily eating dessert.

He had his work cut out for him.

"Nick," Ah Ma said, "you are an expert baker now. Maybe you can even make your own wedding cake!"

"Ah Ma!"

"No, no, of course, you cannot make that yourself. I will do it for you."

"If you try baking something that fancy," Ah Yeh said, "you will surely burn down our house!"

"You're getting ahead of yourselves," Nick said. "I still have to survive dinner with her family. Nobody's getting married anytime soon, despite your boneheaded attempts at matchmaking yesterday."

He didn't admit, however, that he was grateful for the matchmaking shenanigans because he'd gotten to see Lily again.

And he supposed having an audience in the kitchen wasn't the end of the world.

Chapter 8

Lily, her mother, and her sister were sitting around after lunch, drinking tea.

"How did you meet Nick in Toronto?" Ma asked.

"We went on a date last weekend," Lily said. That was accurate enough, wasn't it?

"Then why did you agree to meet Greg yesterday if you were already dating a man?"

"We had been on *one* date, that's all. You can date multiple men at a time, you know, until you decide to be exclusive."

"Hmm," Ma said. "I don't know."

Marla laughed. She was having entirely too much fun with this, enjoying the fact that her antics weren't the topic of conversation for once.

"Did you sleep with him yet?" Marla asked as she took out the apple pie that had been purchased earlier that day. She pulled out a knife and was about to cut herself a piece, but Ma jumped up and grabbed the knife out of her hand.

"No! We must keep the pie looking nice for Nick."

Marla rolled her eyes and helped herself to some cashews instead. "Well, Lily? Are you going to answer my question?"

"I don't know why you think I slept with him."

"Right, because you're the *good* sister. You'd never do anything like sleep with a man after one date."

"Not that there's anything wrong with that," Lily said. "It's the twenty-first century and women can do whatever they like. They shouldn't be judged."

"You definitely slept with him," Marla said, returning to the table.

Lily did not want to lie, so she said nothing.

Marla grinned. "If you've only gone out once, why did you invite him over for dinner?"

"Seemed only fair. I had to meet his family, so he gets to meet mine."

"Sounds petty. I like it."

"I also want Nick to prove he's serious."

"Testing a guy. I like that, too."

"I'm trying to remember what Rosemary told me about Nick." Ma paused. "He is an advertising executive? I think this is correct."

"He has a penthouse." Lily wasn't sure why she'd felt the need to mention that—it made her feel a bit inferior. She had a sip of her tea.

"Ah," Marla said. "It has been confirmed. You went to his place."

"No," Ma said. "Lily could know that without actually going there."

"True, she could, but I think she went to his place."

"I don't see why this matters," Lily said. "Nick and I are dating, and he's coming here for KFC tonight. That's all you need to know."

But she was second-guessing herself. Maybe having him come to Ingleford wasn't the greatest idea after all.

Too late. She'd already invited him. Though she didn't have to cook, she had a list of things to do in preparation—mostly cleaning—and hopefully the house would look as nice as possible.

She couldn't help the nervous excitement flickering in her belly at the thought of seeing Nick again.

He'd show up, wouldn't he? What if he changed his mind?

Nick parked on the street outside a modest brick house in Ingleford. He picked up his plastic containers of butter tarts and date squares—which he'd cut into rectangles because he was a rebel—and climbed out of the car.

He was nervous, if he was honest with himself, and he wasn't used to being nervous about anything in his personal life. For work, occasionally, but not for things like this.

Then again, he'd never met a woman's family before.

He knocked on the door, and a moment later, Lily opened it, looking lovely in jeans and some kind of flowing red shirt. He quite liked her in red, and it reminded him of the day they'd met.

"You came," she said.

He was about to lean in to kiss her, but then another woman skidded into the front hall. She was wearing a band T-shirt and jeans with carefully-placed holes. She studied him in silence for a moment before her face broke into a smile. "Good job, Lily. He looks like Henry Golding."

"That's what I thought the first time we met." Lily turned back to him. "Welcome."

"I'm Marla," said the other woman. "Lily's younger, less uptight sister."

"Marla!" Lily hissed.

"But seriously, good job. This one looks like much more fun than Douglas."

Douglas must be her ex. Hmm.

A middle-aged woman stepped into the hall and approached him with her hand outstretched. "You must be Nick. I am Lily's mother."

"A pleasure to meet you, Mrs. Tseng," he said, hoping he wasn't laying it on too thick.

How was one supposed to act in these meet-the-family situations?

"You brought dessert," she said, eyeing his container. "Lily said you were baking, but I didn't believe her."

"Oh, come on," Marla said. "Men can bake. Just because Dad was allergic to being in the kitchen doesn't mean men can't bake."

They were quiet for a moment, and Nick wondered about Lily's father, but then he looked at her face, and he knew. He just knew.

He slipped off his shoes and followed Lily and Marla into the kitchen while their mother went to get the fried chicken. Lily took his container of sweets and put it on the table, and Marla immediately grabbed a date square. Lily gave her a look.

"What?" Marla said. "I'm hungry, and apparently I'm not allowed to start eating the apple pie." She bit into the date square, and before she finished chewing, said, "Damn, these are good."

"Thanks." Nick smiled. "Do you live in Ingleford?"

"Me? Ha! No, I live in London. For now. I'm a bartender."

"Cool," he said, not sure what the appropriate response was.

"And *you* are dating my sister. I'm not sure why. She's a bit stodgy."

He was taken aback. "Lily is…" Dammit, he was at a loss for words. It was hard to put everything into one or two sentences, especially ones that were appropriate to say in front of her sister. "Definitely not stodgy," he said at last.

Marla barked out a laugh, and he covered Lily's hand with his own.

Dinner went reasonably well. They ate fried chicken, which he hadn't had in a while. The last time had been at one of those Taiwanese fried chicken places that were popping up in Toronto. Maybe he could take Lily to his favorite. Not for a nice date, of course, but if they needed some late-night sustenance, like last weekend.

Mrs. Tseng seemed to like him well enough, thankfully, and she spoke of Lily with great pride. As she should.

After fried chicken, they ate apple pie and butter tarts and date squares, and everyone complimented his baking skills. Lily's moan when she bit into her butter tart was the highlight of the meal, though the way she daintily ate her fried chicken was pretty cute, too.

Note to self: bake for Lily again.

After dinner, she suggested they go for a walk. She led him to a park just off Main Street, and they sat on one of the benches. It was almost like the night before in Mosquito Bay. Her thigh was pressed against his, and when he ran his hand over her leg, she made a sweet little gasp.

"Your father..." he began.

"He passed away three years ago."

"I'm sorry, Lily."

"At first, doing all the holidays without him felt wrong. They weren't happy, certainly not that first year. But now..." She sighed. "It's okay, but I still miss him. He loved KFC Thanksgivings." She pulled out her phone. "This is the closest you can get to meeting him."

She played a voicemail of him wishing her happy birthday and asking her to call back. A short message, but Nick understood why she kept it. Such things could mean a lot after you lost someone.

"That's the only one I have," she said, her voice wobbly.

Nick wrapped his arms around Lily, then pulled her into his lap because he wanted her as close as possible. He kissed her, trying to make everything better for her, though he knew he couldn't. But he wanted to, so badly.

He hadn't known her for long, but her feelings mattered very much to him.

He pulled back so he could see her dark eyes. "Are you heading to Toronto tonight?"

"No, I want to spend more time with my mother. I'm sorry."

"Nothing to apologize for."

"I'm going back tomorrow afternoon."

"When you get back to the city, come to my place. Sound like a plan?"

He needed to be with her again. Alone—not in public, like they were now.

When she smiled tentatively, he pulled her back toward him and set his lips to hers once more, losing himself in the feel of her.

He couldn't make everything perfect for her, but he'd give her what he could.

An hour later, Nick was ready to head home to Toronto, except for one small thing.

He was kissing Lily against the passenger door to his car.

His arms were wound around her, and she wrapped one leg around him, trying to get closer. He was surprised she was making out with him in front of her family's house, but he wasn't complaining.

Earlier, their kisses had been gentler, deeper. Now, it was more desperate. Frantic. He loved all the different kinds of kisses they shared and wanted to experience more with her. He liked variety, but he was discovering he could have that with one woman.

When he squeezed her ass, they both groaned.

He had to step back before this went any further.

"Tomorrow," he said, panting. "I'll see you tomorrow."

A lot had happened since the night they met, and it would be different this time.

He couldn't wait.

Chapter 9

Lily couldn't think straight on her drive back to Toronto that holiday Monday. Normally, she'd be planning the next day in her head, making a mental list of all the things she had to do.

But not today.

No, today she could think only of Nick.

Nick Wong. She knew his last name now.

In fact, she knew a lot of things about him. She'd met his family and saw how he acted around them. He'd met her family. She knew he baked pretty great butter tarts.

She also knew he ate Nanaimo bars in a horrifying way. He always broke off the top chocolate layer and had that first.

Oh, the humanity!

Yet, despite the travesty he'd committed with a Nanaimo bar, she couldn't stop thinking of him, and she ached between her legs, desperate to be with him again. Properly. Somewhere where no one could interrupt them.

When she got to her apartment, she changed into a dress, then texted him to say she was on her way. As she walked to the door of his penthouse—she couldn't believe she was seeing a guy who had a penthouse—she started swaying her hips.

Nick opened the door, wearing dark jeans and a light purple linen shirt—how did he look so good in that? He looked good in everything.

But right now, she had a hankering to see him naked.

He didn't speak, just pulled her toward him and kissed her hard. She fumbled with his shirt, pulling it over his head as the door closed behind them, and ran her hands up and down his gorgeous body. She pressed her lips to his neck and inhaled his clean, soapy scent, then unbuckled his belt and unzipped his jeans.

My God, they hadn't even *said* anything. She was just filling her senses with his body, touching him everywhere she could.

At last, he spoke. "Is being fucked over the counter on your list? Because it's on mine."

"Which list is that?"

"The list of places I want to screw you. It's quite long...ah."

She was touching his cock now, reveling in his reaction. Her power. She'd never felt this kind of power before.

Sure, men had wanted her physically, but never quite like this, and never a man like him.

He pulled away, and before she knew it, he'd bent her over the counter. He lifted up her skirt and shoved her panties down her legs. The air was cool against her slick, heated flesh.

And then the warmth of his mouth on her. He was on his knees behind her, licking her, circling his tongue over her clit.

Then he was gone, and she whimpered in need.

But she could hear him opening a foil packet, and a moment later, he was easing himself inside her. "Tell me if you need me to go slower," he murmured against her neck, growling once he was all the way inside.

She was still wearing her dress. Her stilettos—the same ones she'd worn last weekend. Her panties—well, they were down around her ankles.

This wasn't the kind of sex Lily was used to having, but God, it was good.

He pushed into her again and again. "You're not stodgy at all."

She couldn't help but laugh.

"You're beautiful." He kissed her neck. "Fun." Another kiss. "Maker of delicious Nanaimo bars. Writer of lists."

"Nick?"

"Yes, love?"

"Shut the fuck up."

His chuckle was close to her ear, and he started moving faster inside her; she met him stroke for stroke.

"You're also extremely fun to corrupt," he said.

Yes, this was extremely fun, though she would argue about his use of "corrupt" if she were able to think straight. But she couldn't, not now.

He reached around to fondle her clit, and when she started racing up the last stretch toward her orgasm, he withdrew.

"Nick!" she protested.

"I have other plans for you, don't worry. I'll get you off soon."

He picked her up and carried her into his bedroom, with its large bed and dresser, all in neutral colors...and a large mirror. He positioned her directly in front of the mirror and stood behind her. He slipped the straps of her dress down her arms, followed by the cups of her bra.

"Don't shut your eyes," he whispered. "Watch yourself."

He unclasped her bra and tossed it to the ground. Her breasts popped free, and he massaged the tips between his fingers.

She'd never watched herself in the mirror like this before, and she couldn't help feeling a bit embarrassed at the hard, pink-brown nubs of her nipples, the swell of her breasts. All that bare flesh.

He unzipped her dress and pulled it over her head, then helped her step out of her panties. She was wearing only her heels now.

She watched him kiss her neck and shoulders, closing his eyes as he slipped his hand between her legs and parted her folds. She watched his finger disappear inside her, and oh, God, yes, that was good. With his other hand, he squeezed her breasts and brought her nipple to an even tighter peak.

It was hard to believe this was her, but it was.

Like a sex goddess. That was how he made her feel, and she could see how she was driving him mad, his desperate mouth pressing all over her, his erection pushing against her from behind.

Nick sat down on the bed, grabbed her ass, and brought her down on his cock.

"Fuck!" she said, and nearly covered her mouth in embarrassment afterward. Sure, she swore around people she was comfortable with, but not like that. Never so loudly.

"Now move," he commanded, and she did.

She continued to watch them in the mirror as she rode him. He was behind her; it was mostly herself that she could see.

She touched her breasts, kneading them, plucking the tips. Then she slipped one hand between her legs and touched her clit.

The woman in the mirror gloried in her own pleasure, in her sexuality.

And that woman was *her*.

She rode him, faster and faster, her finger moving quicker on her clit, and when she finally reached the peak and let go, it was like nothing she'd ever experienced before. She sagged against him afterward, like a rag doll, and he pushed into her a few times and came with her name on his lips.

"Lily."

No one had ever said her name the way he did. Like there were so many subtle flavors in it—in her—that she'd never been aware of before.

He wrapped his arms around her and held her close, her bare back against his muscled chest, as she caught her breath.

She continued to look in the mirror, but now she only paid attention to him, to the light perspiration on his forehead, the slight muss of his hair, the way he touched her as if he was in awe of her and wanted to keep her safe at the same time.

"Thank you," she said, lifting herself up from his lap.

"Darling, you don't need to thank me for sex."

"But that time, it was all for me."

"I enjoyed myself too, don't you worry."

He spun her around so she was facing him and not the mirror. Her legs were wobbly; it felt like there was no ground beneath her feet.

"I'm sure you'll find a way to make it up to me," he said with a wink.

There was an odd feeling in her chest, and she could do nothing but lean over and kiss him. His lips were soft but demanding, leading her exactly where she wanted to go. His arms went around her waist and he held her firmly, kept her from falling over.

It was everything.

"I have to tell you something," Lily said later, when they were lying in bed together.

They were eating date squares, and there were several things wrong with this situation.

First of all, they were eating in bed. They would get crumbs in the sheets, surely. She had told Nick of her concerns, but he'd just said to add "eating in bed" to her list of new experiences.

Second of all, he'd cut the date squares—which had been more like rectangles to start with—into triangles to mess with her.

Thirdly, it was close to dinnertime. She should not be eating dessert right before dinner, but that's what was happening.

"What is it?" Nick asked, licking a crumb from the side of his mouth.

"If we're doing this—me and you, I mean—I don't want either of us to see other people." The pain of imagining him giving another woman what he'd just given her... It was too much for her to bear. She knew some people would be fine with it, but she wasn't one of them.

"Of course."

"Of course?"

"I accept your terms," he said. "That's what I'd assumed you'd want."

"And I'd expected you to...I don't know, but you seem to have this sophisticated life of debauchery, for want of a better term, that involves lots of sex."

"My family was calling me 'Mr. Fancypants' when I was baking."

"Mm. I like that."

"I like 'sophisticated life of debauchery.' Good term. And you're the only woman I want right now. I'm more than happy to only have sex with you, don't worry."

He frowned, as though he didn't know what to make of this. But he'd agreed to it, and he'd actually come to Ingleford for Thanksgiving with her family. Plus, he'd baked for her.

She felt a touch naïve, but she trusted him, even though she didn't know quite where this would go, even though she hadn't known him all that long. Although she still had some lingering doubts about whether they really belonged together—they seemed so different—when his arms were around her, she could push those aside.

She laughed.

"What is it?" he asked.

"I'm *terrible* at one-night stands. My first attempt turned into a relationship."

And she couldn't be happier.

Nick didn't usually have trouble sleeping, but that night, he found himself lying awake, listening to Lily's breathing.

Exclusive. She seemed to think that meant they were in a relationship. She'd been pleased, and he hadn't had the heart to question it. He liked making her happy.

But in his brain, "exclusive" and "relationship" weren't equivalent, and he couldn't help feeling a bit uncomfortable with it all. Sleeping with only one woman was one thing, but a relationship... He'd wanted to meet her family to show he could do more than a one-night stand, yes, and he wanted to spend more time with her, but now he felt a little in over his head.

Chapter 10

"So, what have you been up to?" Trystan O'Brien punched Nick lightly on the shoulder.

It was an unseasonably warm October day, and they were sitting on the patio of a downtown watering hole, full of men and women in work clothes. It would likely be the last patio day of the year, and so when Trystan had texted him at five, asking if he wanted to grab a drink, Nick had agreed, rather than staying at the office late like usual.

He considered his answer. He wouldn't lie to Trystan, but his friend would not be impressed with the truth.

"I met someone."

"You...met...someone," Trystan sputtered. "I don't understand."

"I was at Lychee, the Saturday before last."

"I remember. You said you couldn't meet up with me because you were getting laid."

That hadn't been quite how Nick had put it, but yes.

"I overheard a woman say, 'Why is it so difficult to have a one-night stand?' and offered to help with her problem."

"Sounds good so far."

"Then last weekend, my parents arranged dates for me and my siblings for Thanksgiving dinner."

Trystan started laughing. "Desperate to get you guys all married off, are they?"

"Lily—that's her name—was supposed to be Greg's date, but we snuck off together, and my grandma caught us kissing."

Trystan was still laughing.

"Then I went to her family's Thanksgiving. I even made dessert."

"Back up. I missed a few steps. Why did you go to her family's Thanksgiving?"

"To prove I want more than a one-night stand."

Trystan covered his face with his hands and shook his head. "Goddammit. You have a girlfriend now."

Part of Nick wanted to protest at the term, but he didn't.

"Am I going to lose yet another friend to a woman?" Trystan asked.

"You're not losing me as a friend."

"You know what I mean."

Yeah, Nick did.

"Now Saturday will be date night, and on Sunday, you'll go out for brunch." Trystan said the last word quietly, as if it was too horrifying to say in a louder voice.

"What's wrong with brunch?"

"It's the first step on the road to hell."

"Eggs benedict, gourmet waffles, and mimosas are that bad?"

"It starts with brunch," Trystan said morosely. "Next thing you know, she's got a drawer in your dresser and calling you Smoochie Bear."

That reminded Nick of when he'd come across his parents in the kitchen. *Smoochie-boo-kins.* He pushed the unfortunate memory aside.

"And then," Trystan continued, "you're buying her a ring and moving to the suburbs, or back to Mosquito Bay."

Now *that* made Nick shudder.

He'd left Mosquito Bay at eighteen and vowed never to move back. He couldn't imagine Lily wanting to move to Mosquito Bay or Ingleford anyway. She seemed like she belonged in Toronto.

Still, Trystan had made his point.

The thought of a relationship had always made Nick itch. It seemed suffocating, like living in Mosquito Bay, and it felt like the first step to becoming his parents. He loved his parents, despite their fondness for meddling, but he'd known since high school that he wanted a life that was very different from theirs. His parents' lives had always seemed so small and confined, and he had big dreams.

And he'd been living a good life in the city up to now. He didn't want anything that would stop him from being true to himself and reaching his full potential.

He swallowed his unease with a sip of wine.

Despite his fears, Nick was looking forward to his date with Lily on Saturday night. He'd made reservations at Boreal, a Canadian bistro downtown, mainly because of the dessert menu. In fact, he was unreasonably excited about it. Like, the sort of excitement he'd usually feel about a big party—that was how he felt about Lily seeing the dessert list.

Actually, he was excited just to see her.

One of his friends had texted him this afternoon about going to a club tonight, and he'd barely felt any regret about not being able to go.

When he arrived at the restaurant five minutes early, Lily was already there. She sat at a table, her chin resting on her hand, looking out the window. He stood there for a moment, overwhelmed by her loveliness. She was wearing a black shirt that draped in an interesting way, and her hair was wavy tonight, and she was his. There was no chase, no flirting—well, there would be flirting, but it was different now.

Lily turned away from the window, and her face lit up when she saw him. No woman had looked at him quite like that before.

"Hey, Nick." Her eyes traveled down his body, then back to his face. "You look good."

"Oh, this old thing?" he said, tugging the sleeves of his blue suit.

She laughed, and he took a seat across from her.

She was so composed and put together, and he very much liked her look. But he also liked it when she was disheveled and sex-crazed as he fucked her in front of the mirror.

That was the thing about knowing someone for more than a night: you got to see many different sides of them.

He liked all sides of Lily Tseng.

They had a lovely meal together, with a small charcuterie board to start. She ordered the pappardelle with braised lamb, and he ordered the venison with wild mushrooms. They had a reasonably quiet table, tucked into a corner by the window. The lighting was a little dim, and a candle flickered between them.

It was romantic.

He'd done a good job picking this place, even though romance wasn't something he knew much about.

Lily ate her pappardelle delicately. She twirled each wide noodle with care, and she never dared to speak when she had food in her mouth.

He had other things he wanted to do with that mouth.

When the server cleared their plates and asked if they wanted to see the dessert menu, Lily said "no" at the same time as he said "yes."

"Let's take a look." He squeezed her hand.

The server came back a moment later and set a small menu in front of each of them.

"This dessert cocktail looks good," Lily said. "Coffee liqueur and maple syrup and other delicious things. Maybe I'll get one of those."

Maybe she wouldn't see it. Maybe...

"Oh!" She started laughing. "They have a deconstructed Nanaimo bar. I can't believe it! Wait a second... You knew this was on the menu, didn't you? That's why you brought me here."

Busted.

"I did."

He'd never had inside jokes with a woman before, things that were only funny between the two of them. The familiarity made him a little uncomfortable, but her expression was one of delight. Lily's smiles were often a bit restrained, but not now. Not for him.

He couldn't help smiling back at her.

They ordered the deconstructed Nanaimo bar, of course, and Lily ordered the coffee and maple cocktail. She hesitated, probably because of the cost, but he assured her it was no problem.

The dessert came on a long rectangular plate. There was a piece of brown crust in a circular shape, next to a dollop of creamy filling, which was next to a small piece of chocolate. Each component was then repeated, the entire thing covered in chocolate shavings.

"This is wrong," Lily muttered, in a way that suggested she was actually quite pleased. She lifted a forkful of the creamy filling to his lips and he ate it, wishing they were sitting next to each other and he could just lean over and kiss her. Then he broke off a piece of the crust with his fork and fed it to her.

"Mm," she said. "But you know what would be better?"

She scooped up tiny amounts of crust, filling, and chocolate onto her fork.

"You're constructing the deconstructed dessert," he said. "That's against the rules."

"Is it?" She raised an eyebrow. "I had no idea."

"I thought you were a rule follower."

"Most of the time, but then I met you."

They had what he could only describe as "a moment." Everything melted away, even the constructed deconstructed Nanaimo bar on Lily's fork. It was just her and him, and nothing else mattered.

And then, all of a sudden, the world existed again, but it seemed brighter and more brilliant than before.

Lily smiled at him, a little shyly, before sliding her fork into her mouth.

Oh, God. He wanted to kiss her and take off that gauzy black shirt, and he didn't want to let her out of his bedroom until brunch.

It was a little scary, but there was no denying it. He wanted her, and he was terrifyingly glad that she was in his life for more than a night or two.

He helped himself to some of the custardy filling and smiled back at Lily.

This was one date he would never forget.

The next morning, they lay naked in bed, tangled up in the sheets after a round of sex, and Nick wasn't itching to get rid of Lily so he could go about his day and get some work done. No, he was content to be here with her, content to have her lazily trail her fingers over his skin.

Abruptly, she dropped her hand and got up—and he wasn't complaining because he had a nice view of her naked ass as she went to his dresser, picked up a picture that was hiding behind a bottle of cologne, and came back to bed.

"When was this taken?" she asked, pointing at teenage Nick in the family photo.

"I think I was sixteen. It was before Greg went off to university."

She looked between him and the picture. "You look shy! Nick, were you shy?"

"I told you I wasn't cool, didn't I? I was shy, and I hated being different. I felt inferior, got told that girls never went for guys like me and we were supposed to be awkward nerds. Neither of my brothers had that experience—Greg was more or less immune to what everyone else said, and everyone always liked Zach, plus he can pass for being white. But I hated being Asian. Hated my last name. Refused to learn any Cantonese from my grandparents."

He was ashamed he'd felt that way, but he understood how it had happened.

"At last, I got to go to Toronto for school, and I began feeling more comfortable with who I was. I liked being just one more person in a big, diverse city, where nobody knew my family. I started going to the gym, figured out how to project a confidence I didn't feel, and it worked. Three years ago..." He shook his head.

"What?" she asked, setting the picture on the night table.

"I slept with a woman who'd gone to high school with me, who wouldn't have taken a second look at me back then. I'm embarrassed of how proud I was of that, but I did love my new life. Loved that it was nothing like what I would have had back in Mosquito Bay, loved that it was so different from my parents' lives. I never wanted their quiet existence in a gossipy small town, being with the same person for decades..."

Lily worried her bottom lip between her teeth.

Shit. She probably wanted to get married one day and grow old with someone, even if she had no thoughts about the two of them getting married anytime soon.

He glanced at his alarm clock—it was ten thirty. He wanted to do something that would make her smile.

"Let's have brunch," he said in an upbeat voice. His conversation with Trystan popped into his mind, but he pushed it aside. "How do you feel about pancakes? There's a place nearby that's supposed to have the best pancakes with blueberry compote, but I've never been."

"I will gladly eat pancakes with you, Nick, but they better not be deconstructed."

"Don't you worry." He kissed her lips. "I'm sure they will be perfectly constructed."

Chapter 11

It had been three weeks since Thanksgiving, and it had been a very good three weeks for Lily. She'd spent at least one night with Nick every weekend, and several weekday nights with him, too. He texted her at lunch every day. He was surprisingly sweet and thoughtful for a guy who was all about one-night stands.

But somehow, she was special, and he was doing this with *her*.

Still, she had the occasional doubts. He might seem content with what they had for now, but she wasn't convinced he wanted anything long-term, especially after what he'd said when she'd found the old photograph of his family.

Plus, he'd made himself into a man who was smooth and sexy and determined, and she couldn't help feeling a little insecure. If her ex thought she was boring, surely a guy like Nick would eventually come to that conclusion, too. He was a guy who liked variety.

And yet.

The other night, they'd been at a swanky restaurant together. The group of women at the next table had been checking him out, even though he was clearly on a date, and although they were attractive, he hadn't given them a second glance.

No, when he was with Lily, she felt like the only woman who mattered.

Sometimes she wondered if she should be rushing into this when she'd planned to be single for a while, but she pushed those thoughts aside because this was so much fun.

He took her to elegant restaurants and upscale bars. She had to buy new clothes so she didn't appear out of place standing next to Nick, who always looked so fine—she didn't want it to seem like he was way out of her league.

He also brought her coffee in bed and told her about his childhood. She got to know the guy behind the flashy image that everyone knew; he didn't seem to hold anything back from her. She even talked to his mother and grandmother on the phone.

It was good. It was great.

It was just too soon to know if it could go anywhere.

But for the first time in a long time, she was genuinely having fun. She'd never been a person who had lots of fun, but after her father's death, she'd retreated into her routine. Had made herself lists with items like "eat breakfast" and "wash dishes" because crossing out those small things at least gave her something.

Now, however, she could be the responsible career woman during the day and go out with Nick at night.

"Let's go dancing," he said on a Friday night, when they were sitting in his living room.

It was easy to imagine that Nick enjoyed dancing and would be quite good at it, but Lily... Well, this might be a problem.

"I don't dance."

"Surely you dance."

"Not much, and being on a dance floor, surrounded by people who don't look like complete idiots, is intimidating."

"You're good in bed, so you must be good at dancing. It's a fact."

She laughed. "I don't think that's how it works."

He looked at her for a moment. "Okay, no dancing tonight, but tomorrow, one dance—here, at my place—before I leave for the night."

"Yes," she whispered.

Tomorrow, he was going to a charity gala, and she wasn't going with him. He'd told her that he'd love to bring her and surely she'd look lovely all dressed up, but the tickets had sold out months ago, so he had to go alone.

She still hadn't worked out whether she was disappointed or relieved; he seemed disappointed, though.

Just then, his phone rang.

"Sorry, it's my mother," he said before answering. "Hi, Mom... Yes, of course... You already texted me, and I replied, didn't I?... Okay... She is... Sure." He handed the phone to Lily. "She wants to talk to you."

She put the phone to her ear. "Hi, Rosemary, how are you?"

"Lily, I wanted to tell you that I got Shelly Sanderson's coconut lemon square recipe."

"Um, okay?"

"Not that you know who she is, but she makes the best coconut lemon squares and always brings them to the Canada Day picnic, and somehow she left her recipe book in the library. I returned it to her, of course, after I copied that recipe. I don't want anyone to know I have it, but I sent it to Nick, okay?"

Lily held back her laughter. This seemed very...small town. She didn't know what else to call it.

"Nick is supposed to make them for you," Rosemary continued. "If he doesn't, call me and I will have words with him, okay?"

"Okay."

Lily wasn't sure whether Rosemary heard that, however, because there seemed to be a tussle on the other end of the phone. A minute later, a different voice was speaking to her.

"Lily, it's Ah Ma. Nick will make you coconut lemon squares this weekend."

Someone was yelling in the background, presumably Rosemary. "I already told her that!"

"Yes, I heard," Lily said, stifling a laugh.

"Has he proposed yet?"

Ah Ma spoke loudly, and Nick must have heard. He grabbed the phone back from Lily. "We've only been together for a month… Yes, you told me… Stop interfering with my love life… Go bother Greg instead!"

This went on for a while, and Lily couldn't help but smile, though the mention of a proposal had, admittedly, made her a touch uncomfortable.

When Nick got off the phone, shaking his head, he said, "I'll make you coconut lemon squares on Sunday, don't you worry."

He didn't say anything about the rest of the conversation, which was probably for the best.

The next evening, they danced in Nick's living room. He'd asked Lily to wear her red dress, and so she had. He was wearing a tux, and he looked marvelous, of course.

Incredibly dashing. She couldn't take her eyes off him, but all they had was this one dance, and then he would leave.

It reminded her of that scene in *Beauty and the Beast*, except she wasn't wearing yellow and he was no beast. But it was the closest she'd ever come, and it was just the two of them, no one watching her not-so-smoothly move across the floor.

She was falling for him. Oh, God, was she ever falling for him.

And that scared her.

At the end of the dance, he pressed a kiss to her lips, and she nearly melted against him and begged him to take her to bed. But he had to go to the charity gala, and she was meeting Tara and Sam, whom she hadn't seen since the night she'd met Nick.

He walked her over to Lychee, where her friends were having a few cocktails before going out for dinner. Everyone's heads turned to watch them—well, she was positive they were all looking at Nick—as he led her to her friends' table in the lounge area. He kissed her hand, and it was all so ridiculous and over the top, but she loved it.

"Damn," Sam said softly after Nick had left.

Lily jerked her gaze away from the door. "Yeah, I know."

"I thought he was good-looking when I first met him, but *damn*." Sam fanned herself with her hand. "I can't believe you turned your hot one-night stand into something more."

"I can't believe it, either," Lily said, and once she had a cocktail in hand—the same mango and black tea-infused vodka one that she'd had before—she added, "How can this last?"

"Stop it," Tara said. "What's with this lack of self-confidence? You're always poised."

"On the outside, maybe, but I can't help my doubts. He's just too much. He's in a class of his own." Seeing him all dressed up tonight had emphasized that.

"He treats you well, doesn't he?"

"I wouldn't be with him if he didn't. When we're together, everything is perfect, but I can't help worrying. The beautiful playboy who doesn't do relationships is suddenly mine? Like I've tamed him. I shouldn't be thinking about the future yet, but..." She shook her head and had a sip of her drink.

"But what?" Sam pressed.

"His grandma joked about him proposing—or maybe she wasn't joking, I don't know—on the phone yesterday, and it frightened me. Not so much because it was too soon, but because I was disturbed by how much a part of me wanted it, despite the fact that we haven't been together for long. And although our families are a little similar and our mothers are friends, his life is so different from mine. I'm not sure I fit in it."

"Don't overthink this," Tara said. "Have fun and see where it goes."

"I'm not trying to overthink it! But I really like him, and my brain can't help jumping to the future. We're exclusive, but does he even think of me has his girlfriend? I have no idea how serious Nick thinks we are. This isn't what I planned…"

Lily trailed off. She was supposed to be having a fun night out. Time to stop bombarding her friends with her insecurities.

But when she looked at her phone a few hours later, they flooded back.

Chapter 12

Nick hadn't expected to miss Lily quite so much once he was at the gala.

He'd been to a bunch of these events before, and they were always fun. Today, however, he'd spent a full five minutes sulking in the corner with a glass of wine, which wasn't like him.

"Hey, Nick."

He turned. It was a white woman in a purple dress with sequins. Miranda, whom he'd met a couple times before. Last time he'd flirted with her, but she'd told him she had a boyfriend.

There was no denying she was a good-looking woman, but when he saw her now, he didn't feel any lust.

He just wanted Lily, dammit. The worst part was that he'd seen her only a couple hours ago. It wasn't like they'd been apart for weeks.

This was a totally unfamiliar feeling for him.

"Miranda," he said belatedly, giving the woman next to him a smile.

She touched his shoulder, and that was when he knew.

He wasn't accustomed to turning down pretty women, but he wasn't even a little tempted.

"Your boyfriend?" he said when she touched him a second time.

"Not in the picture anymore."

He shoved his hands in his pockets and looked down at his shoes. "But my girlfriend is very much in the picture," he said, surprising himself by saying *girlfriend*.

"Ah." Miranda sounded a little disappointed, but they had a pleasant enough conversation for the next ten minutes.

For dinner, Nick was sitting next to Trystan. The appetizer was something a little fussy but delicious. Nick didn't care, though, because Lily wasn't here to share it with him.

"How's your girlfriend?" Trystan asked with a smirk.

"She's well." Nick paused. "We've had brunch now. Twice."

"I told you, man. Brunch is how it starts. Next thing you know, you're moving to your hometown and chauffeuring a pack of kids in a mini-SUV."

"You have a rather fatalistic view of things," Nick murmured, but this time, he wasn't disturbed by Trystan's dire predictions.

Not because they no longer sounded terrible to him. There was still no way he was going to move to a town like Mosquito Bay or Ingleford. But he'd focused on making his life the exact opposite of his parents', on making people see him as the opposite of how the other kids had seen him in high school.

There were reasons he'd done that. He'd found their small town suffocating, and he'd thought being in a relationship would feel that way, too. He hadn't wanted to be tied to anyone.

Yet belonging to Lily, even though she was more of a "lists and rules" person than he was—that didn't feel suffocating or make his world smaller. Rather, it felt like she'd opened up a new world for him.

One with deconstructed Nanaimo bars and lazy mornings and brunch.

One with an awful lot of sex, it was true.

One with the adventure of learning one person intimately. She got to learn every part of him, too, more than what he showed most of the world.

His parents had been happily married for over thirty-five years, and now he wondered if he might like a life like that after all, but in Toronto.

Even at this fancy event, there was a wonderful ache in his heart. He missed her, and he wouldn't trade it for anything.

He loved her.

He hadn't been looking for this, and yet he'd found it anyway.

Nick left earlier than he normally would, returning to his place around midnight. The lights in his bedroom were on, and Lily was in bed, wearing pajama pants and a low-cut tank top. He'd given her a key so she could come back here after her night out with her friends.

He didn't say anything, just smiled at her.

When he climbed onto the bed and crawled toward her, she returned his smile hesitantly, and he couldn't help wondering why it wasn't her big grin.

"I was..." She shook her head. "You sure look good in that tux."

Then she was kissing him, tearing off his jacket and throwing it on the floor, followed by his tie and shirt. He should hang them up, he really should, but in the end, he left them on the floor.

He pulled Lily's tank top over her head; she wasn't wearing anything underneath. When her bare chest met his, it felt so good, so right.

She unbuttoned his pants, slipped her hand into his boxer briefs, and started pumping him up and down. He needed to touch her, too. He slid his hand under her clothes and ran his fingers over her wetness, loving her response to him.

Normally after an event like tonight's, he'd be having sex, but with a woman he didn't know well, not like his Lily.

His. Yes.

He peeled off the rest of their clothes, then cupped her ass and pressed her against him.

"I really missed you tonight," he said, looking deep into her eyes. He had to make her understand.

"I missed you, too."

She rolled them over so he was on his back, and she took his cock in her mouth. He hissed out a breath. She bobbed up and down, occasionally looking up at him from beneath her pretty eyelashes.

He'd had many women in this bed over the years. He'd enjoyed all of them, but now, he only wanted Lily, could think of no one but her.

She lay down on the bed. "I need you."

Nick rolled on a condom and pushed into her, not wanting to delay any longer.

He moved inside her and kissed her everywhere he could reach. She felt amazing, and he was incredibly lucky that he got to be with her all the time. How had he gotten so lucky?

He licked his finger and circled it over her clit, in the way she liked best. He knew exactly what she liked now, and he loved that. Loved, too, that they could have many different kinds of sex. They'd had that not-so-one-night stand, and he'd fucked her in front of the mirror and watched her discover a side to her sexuality that she hadn't known existed.

Now, she was giving him a kind of sex he'd never experienced before.

Sex with someone he cared for so very much.

She trembled beneath him, close to her orgasm. She never screamed when she came, but her face would open up...just like that.

He came with her, holding her tightly against him.

Yes, this was what he wanted, more than anything.

Something was wrong when Lily woke up the next morning. She tried to sit up, but her body wouldn't obey, and her head felt like shit.

She hadn't drunk that much last night, had she? No, she'd had two cocktails fairly early in the evening, and by the time Nick returned, looking so damn handsome in his tux, she couldn't feel them anymore. They'd had sex before going to sleep. She'd meant to talk to him last night, but she hadn't been able to help herself from jumping him.

Nick wasn't in bed now, but just the thought of sex was unappealing. Her body ached and her head felt like it was stuffed with cotton and her throat was sore. She was definitely sick. Physically sick.

But her heart also ached. She remembered looking at the hashtags for the gala on social media. She'd found lots of pictures of well-dressed people. Nick was in a few of them, looking like he was exactly where he belonged.

She knew she didn't belong in that life.

There was a picture of him standing next to a gorgeous woman in a deep purple dress. Lily had Googled her and discovered she was a high-powered businesswoman.

For now, Lily was a novelty for him, but that would end eventually, and her chest caved in at the thought. This was even worse than being sick.

She collapsed back against the pillow.

A little while later, Nick came in. He was carrying a tray with coffee and—were those the coconut lemon squares that his mother had told her about?

Neither interested her right now. Usually she loved her morning cup of coffee, but not today. Coconut lemon squares weren't normal breakfast food, but of course she would have eaten them if she had any appetite whatsoever.

"What's wrong, Lily?" he asked, setting the tray on the night table.

"I'm not feeling well," she mumbled.

"Oh, no." He put his hand to her forehead. "You have a slight fever."

"I'm not in the mood for coffee and coconut lemon squares, sorry."

"What do you want? I could make wonton soup. I have some wontons in the freezer. Tea? Hot water bottle? Do you need any painkillers?" He looked at her earnestly.

"Wonton soup would be great."

She dozed for a while, until Nick tiptoed into her room with the tray again. This time, it held a large bowl of soup and a glass of orange juice.

He sat on the edge of the bed. "Do you need me to feed you, or can you do it yourself?"

"I'm not *that* sick. I can do it."

He handed her the orange juice. "Vitamin C. You know, I was in China for a business trip once, and they'd heard that North Americans like orange juice for breakfast, so they served Tang. And since it was China, they'd heated it up. Warm Tang."

She laughed at that. Not as much as she usually would, but still.

He did make her laugh, and he was being so sweet right now, looking after her and keeping her company when surely he had better things to do. He had a big job, and he went on business trips to the other side of the world.

Then she berated herself for thinking this was a big deal. All he'd done was bring her a small meal in bed when she wasn't feeling well. It was a natural thing to do when you cared for someone, but perhaps Douglas had taught her to have low expectations when it came to men.

She was still afraid, but maybe she should just talk to Nick.

"I have something to tell you. I…"

She stopped when she heard someone pounding on the door.

Chapter 13

With a sigh, Nick got up from the bed and headed to the door.

He knew exactly who it was.

This happened once or twice a year. His family, bored in Mosquito Bay, would spontaneously decide to drive to Toronto and show up for a visit.

Last time, a woman had just been leaving his penthouse, and that had been...interesting.

This time, there was a sick woman in his bed, and he wanted to focus on her, not his family.

He opened the door.

Mom, Dad, Ah Ma, and Ah Yeh shouted, "Surprise!"

He pinched the bridge of his nose. "You know it's not my birthday."

"Of course we know. Don't be silly," Mom said. "We're taking you out for dim sum! Greg will meet us at the restaurant."

"This isn't the best time. Lily—"

"Lily can come with us!" Ah Ma said gleefully. "We will ask her lots of questions. Make sure you have been treating her well."

"Lily is sick," he said. "She's in my bedroom."

"Oh, no," Mom said. "What does she have? Is it the flu?"

"You must not give her anything cold," Ah Ma said. "No ice water! Warm water is best."

"I just made her soup."

"I want to see her," Mom said. "Make sure she's doing okay."

"Me, too," Ah Ma said.

Dad shook his head. "I don't want you to catch anything, Ma. You should stay away from sick people."

"Aiyah. How do you think I got so old? I am invincible!"

"You are eighty-seven. You are not invincible."

"I am eighty-eight!"

"No," Dad said, "you're eighty-seven."

"Eighty-eight. Lucky age!"

"I thought you said you had one foot in the grave?"

This was giving Nick a headache. "Look, could you please quiet down?"

Ah Ma marched into his place, not even bothering to take off her shoes, and went straight to his bedroom. Having been here several times before, she knew exactly where to go.

"Lily!" she said when she reached the bedroom door, Nick right behind her. "You are sick, I hear? Good thing Ah Ma is here to take care of you."

"I'm fully capable of doing it myself," Nick said.

"Wah, is that cold orange juice I see? Why you always serve juice cold?"

"Because it tastes weird when it's warm."

"I will make jook."

"No," Ah Yeh said. "I make better jook than you."

"I can cook chicken noodle soup," Mom suggested.

Lily looked exhausted, and she'd been about to tell Nick something important when his family barged in. Goddammit.

"No, no, it's okay," Lily said. "You said you were going to have dim sum? Go ahead. I'll be fine here for a couple hours."

"We will bring him back to you soon!" Ah Ma promised. "Then I will take care of you."

"No," Dad said. "You're old. People should be looking after you, not the other way around."

"Fine." She stuck her nose in the air. "Carry me!"

"I'm not carrying you!"

"Please," Nick said, "let's allow Lily to finish her food in peace and maybe get some more sleep. I'll go out for dim sum, but I won't stay long, okay?"

"Are these coconut lemon squares?" Mom was already in the kitchen. "You made them this morning? They look fresh."

"I did."

"Coconut lemon squares are not good for sick people," Ah Ma said. "Too much sugar."

"Unless *you* make them," Ah Yeh said. "You used salt instead of sugar."

"Too much salt is bad, too."

"Obviously! They were inedible."

Once Nick had finally herded his family out the door, he returned to Lily. "Are you sure you're okay if I go out for an hour or two?"

"Yes, don't worry. I'll be fine."

"Text me if you need anything. You can tell me whatever you need to tell me when I get back. I'm sorry about this."

Lily alternately fretted and slept as she waited for Nick to return from dim sum with his family. They appeared to have the uncanny ability of arriving just at the wrong time.

She was about to text Tara when she heard the door open.

Her heart kicked up a notch, like when he'd returned from the charity gala last night. Except now she was sick and filled with more self-doubt.

"Hey," he said as he walked into the room. "How are you doing?"

Often she felt a spark of lust when she saw him, but not today. Her body was in no mood for anything but staying in bed and shuffling to the kitchen and bathroom.

But she smiled because she couldn't help it when she saw him. He'd made her feel safe from the very first night he'd taken her home.

The thought of losing him, the thought that she might not be enough for him...

He sat down on the bed and clasped her hands in his.

"I don't want to give you my germs," she said.

"I don't care."

He might care if his body felt the way hers did right now, but she didn't say that.

"I saw lots of pictures of you at the gala," she began. "You looked like you were on the red carpet at the Oscars. So polished, probably paying a thousand bucks or more for your ticket. And I'm an ordinary woman. I'm not rich; I'm not even interesting. I don't belong in your world. When it was just for a night, I could push that aside, pretend it was no big deal, but now..." Tears pooled in her eyes, but she didn't let them fall.

"Lily," he murmured, wrapping his arms around her. "Oh, Lily."

"When we're together, it's wonderful, and you've always been good to me. And yet..."

"I'd never even had a girlfriend until I met you."

So he did think of them that way. Still...

"Maybe," she said, "you wouldn't have one now if you weren't jealous that I'd been set up with your brother." The words were bitter in her mouth, but they came out anyway.

"I admit I was jealous, but even if the circumstances had been different, I can't stay away from you. After our first night, I kept thinking about you. Last night at the gala, more than anything, I wished you were there with me."

He stretched out on the bed next to her and held her more tightly.

"I just worry," she said quietly, "that someday you'll get bored of me."

"I will never get bored of you."

"My ex broke up with me because he found me boring, which is why I made a list of new things to try—including a one-night stand. I told you that, didn't I?"

"Your ex is an ass," Nick said, with quite a lot of passion. "Truly, I could never find you boring. I think you were just stuck in a bit of a rut."

She nodded. "It was tough after my dad passed away."

"You did what you had to do to get through it, and for you, that meant following a tight routine and never stepping outside your comfort zone. There's nothing wrong with that."

"Plus, I've always been the well-behaved daughter. The one who didn't get in trouble. And now…" She trailed off as she realized something. "With you, I feel like myself. I do. I just can't help worrying that your life has gotten less snazzy and fast-paced with me in it."

He sat up and took her hands in his. He looked into her eyes like she was the only thing that mattered. "I don't want my life to be exactly as it was before. It's not the same with you in it—and that's a good thing. I like what I have with you."

She managed an inelegant sniffle. "You're serious about us? You're not afraid of long-term relationships?"

"I admit I was a bit uncomfortable with the idea a few weeks ago, but not now." Nick cupped her face in his hands and swept his thumbs over her cheeks. "I love you, Lily. I always knew I didn't want the life my parents had in Mosquito Bay, and I did my best to make sure my life was nothing like theirs. But now, what I want more than anything is to be with you, and please never call yourself boring because it's not true, not at all. I want to learn every little thing about you. I'm fascinated by the strange way you eat Nanaimo bars—"

"I eat them like a normal person! None of your one-layer-at-a-time crap."

"—and by the way you eat fried chicken so daintily."

"I do not!"

He smiled. "You totally do, and it's cute. I'm fascinated by the noises you make when I'm inside you—and the way you're blushing now. I love how you're so careful and aware of everything around you but completely uninhibited in my arms. There's a freckle on the back of your earlobe, did you know that? I love that, too. And you've already met my family and haven't run away screaming. I want to have lots of new experiences with you, and although I'm never going to be the man who has a quiet life in a small town—"

"Don't worry, I don't want that either."

"I know." He paused. "I don't need the whirlwind that I've been living for the past decade, and to be honest, when I look back on it, it seems like a rather shallow life. I want exactly what we have together. Please don't feel like you're not good enough just because of my money and 'snazzy' life. That means nothing compared to what I feel for you, Lily, and it certainly doesn't mean we don't belong together. God, no. I've been lucky in life, and if I lost all that but had you, I would still count myself lucky."

He slid his hands to her shoulders and looked into her eyes. She couldn't doubt the sincerity in his words, in his touch.

"To be honest," he said, "sometimes I think *I'm* not good enough for you, especially with my lack of experience in this area. Try not to let those feelings overwhelm you. I'll reassure you whenever you need it, and we don't have to go to galas if they make you uncomfortable."

Lily nodded. She was doing a strange combination of hiccupping and sobbing, and he didn't tell her to stop, just handed her a tissue.

She wasn't at her best. She tried to look put together most of the time, but now she was sick and wearing pajamas, and he'd declared his love for her all the same. Much of the past few weeks had been full of exciting new experiences—well, not all of them were new, but they felt new because she was doing them with Nick Wong.

But he didn't just want her in the busy moments. He wanted her in the quiet moments, too. He wanted all of her.

"Although my past doesn't show my ability to commit," he said, "I am definitely committed. Here, I got you something as proof."

He picked up a container she hadn't noticed before. It was emblazoned with the logo of the dumpling place they'd gone to that first night.

She laughed.

"I believed in love before," he said, "but I never thought it would be part of my life, and now... Well, I wasn't even tempted to eat these on the walk home, that's how much I care for you."

"You weren't tempted? What are you, a monster?"

He chuckled. "Okay, maybe I was a little tempted."

Lily wasn't sure she'd ever loved any gift as much as she loved these soup dumplings. Soup dumplings were pretty amazing on their own, but these were extra amazing because they'd come from Nick and they were just for her.

"I'm not sharing." She placed a protective hand over the dumplings.

"You don't need to."

She opened the container and took the pair of chopsticks he handed her. God, these smelled good. She didn't have a huge appetite today, but her stomach rumbled, and as she looked from Nick to the soup dumplings and back to Nick, her insides turned to...well, soup.

"I love you, too," she whispered. "I was just scared that you didn't feel the same way and that I was foolish for giving my heart to a guy who was supposed to be a one-night stand. I'm sorry for being insecure—"

"You don't need to apologize for anything. I'm glad you told me, and I will make sure you never forget how much I care."

"I can't believe I'm sick for such a romantic moment."

"The kisses and sex can wait until another day, don't worry."

"You know what? Lemon is good for sick people, isn't it? I think I might fancy a coconut lemon square, Mr. Fancypants."

He laughed before getting up. He returned a minute later with a coconut lemon square—

Wait. It was actually two coconut lemon triangles. He'd cut the square in half.

Silly Nick.

It was a side of him she hadn't seen right away, but she quite liked it. The side of him that had wanted to take her to Boreal specifically for its deconstructed Nanaimo bars. She chuckled at the memory.

He sat down on the bed and positioned her so she was sitting between his legs. He wrapped his arms around her as she devoured her food, and she was so full of love that she even let him have one of her dumplings.

The next day, she was completely better. Love and soup dumplings and coconut lemon triangles must have worked their magic.

While her boyfriend was in the shower, she wrote "fall in love with Nick Wong" on her list, then immediately crossed it out because it had already happened.

The following Saturday, Nick and Lily spent a quiet hour wandering the greenhouses at Allan Gardens. Lily suspected this was the sort of thing Nick never would have done in the past, but here they were.

Later, they went to Lychee together, and this time, they sat in the restaurant instead of the lounge. This time, the man sitting across from Lily wasn't someone she'd just met, but someone she knew well, someone she was looking forward to knowing even better, someone she was looking forward to building a life with.

This time, Operation Get Laid Tonight was a sure thing.

And this time, Nick didn't profess his talent for one-night stands.

Instead he said, "Being with you, Lily Tseng, is my specialty," and she believed him with all her heart.

After all, he'd brought her soup dumplings, and that was a pretty big sign of love.

Epilogue

It was December 23, and Nick was back in Mosquito Bay with Lily. He wouldn't normally have come back this early—usually he'd arrive on Christmas Eve and return to Toronto on Christmas Day—but this time, the two of them were spending a few days here. For whatever reason, being in his hometown didn't make him quite as uneasy as it had in the past.

Not that he would ever move back here, of course.

Instead, Lily was planning to move into his place in Toronto sometime in the next few months, and he couldn't wait. They already spent so much time together, and he wanted to have her there on a permanent basis.

Last Christmas, he would have laughed at the thought of being in a committed relationship, but now, it felt right. It felt like what he was meant to do.

It had been almost three months since he'd met Lily, and she'd changed his life. Not that he regretted how he'd lived before, but this was better, even if Trystan was disappointed in him for giving up his bachelor lifestyle and going out for brunch regularly.

He turned to Lily, who was snuggled up next to him on the sofa, and smiled.

As always, the sight of her made his heart soar.

"Dinner's almost ready." Dad came into the living room, where Nick, Lily, Zach, Amber, Ah Yeh, and Ah Ma were sitting. There were no blind dates today. Not yet, anyway. Or maybe the blind dates would show up on Christmas Eve—it was tough to say.

Nick's family was thrilled that he and Lily were together, and they were trying to claim credit for the match, even though they'd set Lily up with Greg, not Nick.

Speaking of his older brother...

"Greg still isn't here?" Dad asked.

Nick shook his head, then glanced out the window. "It's really coming down out there."

The storm wasn't supposed to have started yet, but it had been snowing pretty hard for a while now, and his brother was out on the road. Hopefully he was almost here.

Just then, Nick's phone vibrated.

"It's from Greg," he said slowly as he read the text. "He says the 402 is closed and he had to stop at a motel for the night...and he's with Tasha? I don't understand."

"He's driving Tasha back from Toronto for the holidays," Ah Ma explained. "They will be staying at a motel together? Oh, this is great news!"

Nick stared at his grandma as understanding dawned.

More matchmaking games were afoot in his family, and he wondered if his parents and grandparents were secretly capable of controlling the weather.

It wouldn't surprise him.

But for now, his brother was safe, and Nick was with Lily. He was looking forward to eating the Nanaimo bars they'd made earlier. Maybe he'd ask her to lick out the creamy filling and eat all three layers separately. Maybe he'd kiss her afterward.

Well, he'd most certainly do that.

It would indeed be a wonderful holiday.

About the Author

Jackie Lau decided she wanted to be a writer when she was in grade two, sometime between writing "The Heart That Got Lost" and "The Land of Shapes." She later studied engineering and worked as a geophysicist before turning to writing romance novels. Jackie lives in Toronto with her husband, and despite living in Canada her whole life, she hates winter. When she's not writing, she enjoys gelato, gourmet donuts, cooking, hiking, and reading on the balcony when it's raining.

To learn more and sign up for her newsletter, visit jackielaubooks.com.

Also by Jackie Lau

Love, Lies, and Cherry Pie

Donut Fall in Love Series
Donut Fall in Love
The Stand-Up Groomsman

Weddings with the Moks Series
Four Weddings to Fall in Love
Three Reasons to Run

Chu's Restaurant Series
The Sitcom Star
The Reluctant Heartthrob

Kwan Sisters/Fong Brothers Series

Grumpy Fake Boyfriend

Mr. Hotshot CEO

Pregnant by the Playboy

Bidding for the Bachelor

Cider Bar Sisters Series

Her Big City Neighbor

His Grumpy Childhood Friend

Her Pretend Christmas Date (novella)

The Professor Next Door

Her Favorite Rebound

Her Unexpected Roommate

Holidays with the Wongs Series

A Match Made for Thanksgiving

A Second Chance Road Trip for Christmas

A Fake Girlfriend for Chinese New Year

A Big Surprise for Valentine's Day

Baldwin Village Series

One Bed for Christmas (prequel novella)

The Ultimate Pi Day Party

Ice Cream Lover

Man vs. Durian

Chin-Williams Series

Not Another Family Wedding

He's Not My Boyfriend

www.ingramcontent.com/pod-product-compliance
Lightning Source LLC
Chambersburg PA
CBHW031517010826
48973CB00013B/2635